THE SPIDER:
THE SPIDER AT BAY

MASTER OF MEN!

THE SPIDER AT BAY

By Grant Stockbridge

POPULAR PUBLICATIONS • 2022

CHAPTER 1
INTO THE TRAP!

RACING THE stolen police car along the twisting mountain road, Richard Wentworth kept a sharp lookout on his back trail. Twice, in the long dash from Albany, he had been sure the pursuit of the Black Police was shaken off. But each time their headlights, menacing as the fierce eyes of some wild beast, appeared once more, doggedly ferreting out his flight. They were no more than a mile behind now and, despite the wide-open roar of Wentworth's engine, they were creeping closer.

Wentworth turned his keen, bitterly intelligent eyes to the road ahead. He was within five miles of safety, but it was a sanctuary he dared not claim unless he first shook off these minions of the organized criminals who, in these mad days, controlled the state government. Many brave men, whole families of fugitives from the tyranny and cruelty of the Black Police, were quartered in this hideout. If he fled there, they would be betrayed.

Once more, Wentworth flung a glance backward. That pursuing car was much closer. His lips straightened in a thin line. It was always like this now when he made his forays against the tyrants. There must be fully a hundred thousand of the Black Police under arms and ceaselessly patrolling roads and city streets. The people were frantic—terrified. They had been stripped of their wealth, even the poor of their stern necessi-

1

ties, by tax collectors who used the extortion methods of rack-
eteers....

Wentworth laughed harshly. His own wealth had been figured
in millions, long since dedicated to the service of the people, as
his own life had been since youth. He had risked everything a
hundred times in battles against the underworld, but now the
situation was reversed. The underworld was on top. It was in the
saddle, in complete control of state and city machinery. And,
ironically, it had been the people themselves who had put the
criminals in power! The election had been legitimate enough

Some stood unflinchingly before the lifting rifles—others cowered in prayer.

despite the lavish expenditure of campaign funds, and for that reason the Federal government had been powerless to intercede. All this crime was committed with the full sanction of the law and the courts!

Take Wentworth's own case. Charged with being the Spider—that was the identity under which, through the years, he had fought the underworld, but not always within the law—Wentworth had been declared a public enemy, an outlaw. Under a new state law, his entire wealth had been impounded pending trial. On the surface, only that had happened. Actually, Wentworth knew, his wealth had long since flowed into criminal coffers!

But he dared not face trial. Those judges who refused to obey the mandates of the new government had been rapidly disposed of—within the law. One by one, they had been impeached by subservient legislators. And there was no redress save in the way Wentworth had chosen, the furtive raids in the black of night, the recourse of men who were outlawed because they were honest!

PERHAPS IT was because of his bitter thoughts that Wentworth had no warning of the trap into which he drove. It had been carefully set. He rounded the sharp curve of the hill road where a shoulder of Old Baldy Mountain crowded it close against the brawling waters of Rocky River. As his headlights jerked back to the roadway, he saw the barricade, not fifty feet away. Built solidly of tree trunks, it blocked the entire passage between rocky wall and the brawling cataract. Even as he spotted the trap, he was blinded by the broad, intense beams of military searchlights blazing into his eyes. But before that he had caught the steely glint of leveled rifles!

There was no time for thought, scarcely time to act, but the Spider had not survived a thousand battles with the underworld by sluggish reaction to danger. His reflexes were acutely attuned. Despite the drain of sleepless nights and constant exertion, his body was in perfect physical condition, his brain razor keen. In that split-second, he had estimated his chances and made his choice.

Even as the dazzling light struck him like a violent blow, he wrenched the auto from the road and sent it lunging toward the turbulent river. With the same movement, he flung himself crouching, flat on the floor, putting the maximum protection between his body and those lean-snouted rifles.

Instantly, the night was torn apart by a crashing volley of the rifles and, louder than their blast, riding it as thunder rides a storm, the chattering fury of a machine gun rolled out. The storm of lead struck the car with the violence of a suddenly released hurricane. It shuddered, swerved in its course. Glass pelted down upon Wentworth's back and bullets struck on the metal body like a titan's drum roll. If there had been time for a second volley, nothing could have saved Wentworth. But the speed of his car had been terrific. As the bullets struck, the front wheels crashed the rocks on the river's margin and it leaped like a heart-shot deer and crashed down into the dark flood.

Wentworth felt the upward, lurching surge of the car as it left the bank, and his hand leaped to the door at his head. An instant later, he was tumbling through space, then the icy water

swallowed him. Swimming was
out of the question. Half-stunned
by the violence of the plunge, his
muscles contracted by the knif-
ing cold, Wentworth was swept
brutally down the stream. A rock
sledged against his ribs. Then he
was sinking in the deep pool at the

bottom of the cataract, sinking and racing on with the swift,
mountain current which flowed deep and fiercely at this point.

Even half-conscious as he was, Wentworth's keen brain was
working. The Black Police would not be content with hoping
that he had been killed in that crash. Within moments, they
would be streaming along the river's banks with ready guns!
Wentworth fought the paralysis of the cold, which already was
cramping his limbs; and struggled against the numbing effect
of the shock. Slowly, he forced himself to movement. The rapid
thrust of the river already had carried him nearly a quarter of a
mile below the barricade. At intervals, he managed to bob his
head above water long enough to breathe, but he realized he
was nearly spent.

A dark shadow, slanting out from the bank, indicated a fallen
tree, and Wentworth managed to maneuver so that his weary
body collided with it. Minutes seemed to pass before he could
drag himself, with its help, to the bank and clamber ashore. He
staggered into the woods that grew close, at this point, to the
river. Behind him, men were shouting. He could hear the crashing of their progress through the underbrush as they searched

the banks for him. Wentworth braced himself against a tree, removed the twin automatics from their clips beneath his arms, reloaded them with fresh bullets from a water-tight packet in his pocket—then he pushed on.

THERE WAS the sharp crease of a frown between his arched brows. He knew now why the car, which apparently he had lost, had been able to reappear on his trail. Obviously, he had been followed on his other trips into the mountains. The barricade proved that the Black Police had known the course he would take. He stopped abruptly, alarm tingling his brain. If they already knew his course, they must also know the location of the cavern sanctuary in the hills!

With that thought, new resolution put strength into Wentworth's body. Even the biting cold of the thin mountain air scarcely chilled him. He had to reach the camp at once, evacuate the people there… Wentworth checked his retreat and peered about to get his bearings. Against the star-glittering sky, he could make out the shoulder hunch of Old Baldy. The sanctuary was beyond that, five miles. If it were not already too late, he would soon get there—in one of the Black Police cars from beyond the barricade! It was sound strategy. Whatever those ambushers might expect, they would certainly not look for him to attack!

The automatics balanced in his hands, Wentworth moved softly to meet the men who were hunting him down. The mouth that could be so kind was now pressed into a harsh gash strangely like that of the Spider's accustomed disguise.

There would be no mercy for these Black Police when his

guns spoke. They had been recruited from the cells of prisons, from the dregs of the underworld. Too often, Wentworth had seen them torturing helpless citizens who happened to oppose them. Wentworth froze and shrank against the black bole of a tree. The gleam of a flashlight had shone through the shrubbery and two of the Black Police, automatics in hand, plodded along the bank of Rocky River.

"He won't come up till doom's day," one of them said, and laughed roughly. "We put enough lead in his carcass to sink him clear through the bottom to China!"

"Maybe," the other one grunted. "Gawd knows I hope so. But the chief said not to take no chances."

Wentworth waited until they were nearly opposite the place where he crouched, then he stole toward them. If he could capture them soundlessly… But it was necessary to move too fast for absolute quiet. One of the two police cursed and whirled toward him. In a single, lithe leap, Wentworth reached the man's side, and the automatic in his left hand swung in a chopping, blurred arc. The sound of its striking was solid as an ax biting into oak.

The second man flung up his gun and fired wildly. Wentworth's catapulting dive drove his shoulder against the man's chest in the next instant, sent him hurtling backward into the river. A choked cry, a splash swiftly smoothed by the fast-moving current, and the policeman was gone. Wentworth bent over the man he had slugged and swiftly changed garments with him.

Afterward, he tossed the body, clad in his own clothing, into the river. It was not murder. Wentworth's heavy blow with the automatic had crushed out his life instantly....

One uniformed man, automatic in hand, stood guard over the three police cars parked in the woods road just beyond the barricade. He lounged against a tree, smoking. Abruptly, he snapped to the alert.

"Stop right there!" he snarled. "Who in the hell are you?"

Clad in police clothes, Wentworth stepped from the darkness. "Pipe down," he returned in the same tone. "Who'd you think it was, Governor Whiting?"

The guard relaxed—and that was a mistake. The next instant, a fist was buried in his solar plexus and another clicked home against his jaw. Wentworth stood frowning down at the guard, shook his head. He had no time to bind the man—and those blows had been solid.

He swung to the police car nearest the road, set it rolling downgrade with its motor dead, presently let out the clutch so that the engine caught without the whirring of the starter. Throttling along dead slow, he crept away from the barricade. But presently he moved more rapidly. Usually, he left the road and walked the last mile to the sanctuary, but tonight, there was no time. He might already be too late. If he were, he would be rushing into another ambuscade....

WENTWORTH WRENCHED the car into an opening in the close underbrush of the woods, rolled through a fringe of trees and across an open pasture. A shallow stream, carefully cleared of boulders, made him a roadway for a half mile, then he swung the car up a steep climb, began to wind between forest trees. The road here was well defined. Abruptly, men burst from the underbrush on each side. Light blazed into his face, and there were glittering guns.

Relief made laughter pump from Wentworth's throat. "Thank God I'm in time!"

"It's the commander!" one of the men in the darkness cried. "Hey, send the word! The commander is here!"

Wentworth thrust from the car and eyed a powerful man. Now that the lights were out, the high glitter of the stars limned him fairly, broad-shouldered, bearded, his head surmounted by a clean turban.

"The *missie sahib* said you would come, *sahib*," he whispered. "We have waited the feast."

Wentworth's lips relaxed a little from their battle grimness. The Hindu warrior who walked beside him was his own personal servitor in normal days, and had now been set as a guard over Wentworth's fiancée, Nita van Sloan. She had been forced into hiding also, for the Black Police did not scruple to attack a man through his loved ones. She had been expecting him.

"The feast?" he said curiously. "I don't understand, Ram Singh."

Ram Singh's deep voice was quiet, contented now that his master was beside him. "It is the feast you call Thanksgiving, *sahib.*"

A startled exclamation was surprised from Wentworth. Had it really been three months since they had been forced to flee into the hills? It was already Thanksgiving. He smiled faintly. There would be no feast tonight. A hurried meal, then flight…

At the carefully muffled entrance of the cave, Nita van Sloan ran into his arms and he caught her fiercely to him. Their meetings had been all too few in these perilous months.

"I knew you'd come if you could," she said. "Oh, Dick!"

In the central cavern, which they reached after a quarter mile scramble through narrow ways, a fire blazed on a great central hearth, its fumes sucked upward through a ceiling vent. There were a hundred men and women about the chamber, and they sprang to their feet at the sight of him. A cheer rang through the vaults. Wentworth lifted his hand for silence.

"I bring you bad news," he said quietly. "I'm sorry that it falls out so tonight. I was ambushed by the Black Police five miles from here, just above where the road crosses Rocky River. It can only mean that they have located our hideout!"

A stocky man with a weather-reddened face strode forward, his shoulders rocking with the roll of a seaman.

"We can fight them off, sir," he said, deep-voiced. "Just give me five men and go on with the dinner."

Wentworth smiled. "I don't doubt it, Sailor Joe," he said quietly, "but the value of any one of our encampments obviously is lost when it's discovered. I want a volunteer group of men. A dozen will be enough...."

Before he had finished speaking, every man in the chamber was on his feet, volunteering even before they knew the task that lay ahead of them. Wentworth paused for their shouting to die before he could speak, but there was pride in him. A few short weeks before, these men had been grocers, clerks, skilled workmen. Discipline and work had turned them into a closely-knit corps of fighting men, more efficient by far than the sloppy criminal Black Police.

Not one of them but owed his life and the lives of his loved ones to Wentworth and the men he captained. How could men such as these long be defeated by criminal tyranny, Wentworth asked himself—and not for the first time. Nowhere in the world were men so free, so liberty-loving as here in his native America. Nowhere would they fight so fiercely for justice and right. Yet they were failing. Three months now they had tried without success to track down and destroy the Master behind the criminals. A few successful raids, yes, but criminals still ruled… Wentworth shook the thought from his mind.

"Sailor Joe," he said, "choose a dozen men and… eliminate the Black Police who ambushed me. It's barely possible they're the only ones who have tracked us this far. Bring the bodies and all supplies back here."

Sailor Joe touched his forelock, grinning. "Aye, aye, sir," he growled. "Landing-party this way! All right, you volunteers!"

"Joe," Wentworth called, "they have rifles, at least one machine gun and Army searchlights."

Sailor Joe rubbed his grizzled jaw. "And we could use another machine gun," he said. "Hey, you lubbers. The Black Police are donating another machine gun!" The party he had chosen filed out through the narrow entrance of the cavern and the echoes of their footsteps died out. Wentworth turned to Nita.

"I think I've got a cracked rib," he said. "If you'll get some bandages…" He turned to the assembled crowd. "Go on with your meal," he said. "We won't have long."

12

HE WALKED off with Nita. "The safest measure is to evacuate at once. We can leave a watch behind to find out if this place is discovered. Later, perhaps we can return."

"Any luck in Albany?" Nita asked quietly while she prepared bandages.

Wentworth frowned. "I think I've figured out a way to get hold of Governor Whiting. I know he's not the brain behind this thing, but perhaps he can be forced to talk if we brought him... or to one of the other camps. How did the rebellion in Titustown come off?"

Nita's face was pale as she inspected the bruise on Wentworth's side and her cool fingers prodded to find the extent of the injury.

Wentworth winced, and Nita looked up at him apprehensively. Her cheeks were tanned from the out-of-door life to which she had been driven, but the soft violet depths of her eyes were the same and the chestnut curls clustered about her oval face. Wentworth looked into her eyes, and she glanced away.

"It's just a fracture," she said. "No actual separation. Some adhesive...."

Wentworth cupped her chin in his hand, "Things went... badly in Titustown?" he asked quietly.

Nita smiled faintly at him. "Very badly, Dick," she said. "There was a slip-up, or a leak. The Black Police raided the arms depots an hour before the rebellion, and crushed it."

Wentworth swore softly. "I knew I should have gone myself!" he cried. "What about Kirkpatrick?"

Nita shook her head. "There's no word of him."

Wentworth jumped to his feet, but Nita forced him to a seat again while she strapped up his injured side. She knew how close was the friendship of the two men, Wentworth and Stanley Kirkpatrick, who had been ousted from the police commissionership of New York City after years of faithful service.

They had often been on different sides of the law, Wentworth and Kirkpatrick, but always they had struggled toward the same goal—the protection of the people from criminals. Kirkpatrick had long been convinced that Wentworth was the Spider, whose swift justice struck where the law could not reach. It was fortunate that he had never been able to assemble the evidence to prove it, for Kirkpatrick would never have swerved from the course of absolute duty—even for such a friend as Wentworth. And now, Kirkpatrick, too, was outside the law, branded a public enemy by the criminal courts, his property confiscated. There was a ten-thousand-dollar reward on his head for capture, dead or alive....

"Wait, Dick," Nita pleaded. "Wait until I have finished with the bandage."

"There must be some word," Wentworth said quickly. "Nita, what are you holding back? If you knew the revolt failed—"

"Wait," Nita urged again, and would not speak until she had finished the job. Then she stood quietly before Wentworth, with her violet eyes on his. "There is nothing anyone can do now," she said. "The Black Police have taken over the entire city. They are going to make an example of it. More than fifty executions, half the population shifted to concentration camps and a fine of two million dollars on the business men."

Wentworth sprang to his feet. "They can't be allowed to do that!" he cried fiercely. "I'll go myself."

"Please, Dick," Nita urged. "You can't… There's more bad news."

"More!"

Nita nodded slowly. "Some horrible disease has broken out in Titustown. Some awful thing like leprosy, but it kills quickly, terribly."

"The Black Police," Wentworth whispered the words fiercely. "They're behind it! They're bound to be. New diseases don't develop overnight. God, if I could get my hands on the Master!"

"But it's too late, Dick!" Nita pleaded. "The whole city is surrounded. In the morning, the executions and the evacuation starts. Besides, you have to get these people to safety. And that disease…" Wentworth smiled and clasped her shoulders in his hands. "I can't desert them, Nita," he said. "Don't forget, *I urged them to revolt!*"

"But, Dick, the state needs you! No one else can hold the men together, make the plans! Kirkpatrick will do everything that can be done in Titustown!"

"I'm going," Wentworth said. "And I'll go alone. We have enough men there for any work. No use endangering more lives. You take charge of the evacuation here. Heavy arms and equipment must be hidden and hidden well. Disband the group and scatter it. They must make their way to the Catskill camp."

Nita was silent for a long moment, then she forced a smile to her lips. "I knew you'd go, Dick," she said, "but I hoped you could stay for a little while… I'm not really a coward, Dick!"

"You're brave, dear," Wentworth told her. He caught her fiercely into his arms, then strode to the crowded fireside again. "I leave Miss van Sloan in charge," he cried. "You must evacuate at once."

He started toward the entrance of the chamber, and men cried out to stop him. "Stay with us, commander! We'll fight them off!"

Wentworth paused for a moment in the exit. The firelight was warm on his stern-lined, pleasant face, showed the tired lines about his compressed lips. But his shoulders were erect and his gray eyes showed their rigid and inflexible purpose. A tall man, with a deceptive slightness of build that did not reveal the whip-cord strength of that finely trained body. Command sat easily on his shoulders, and it was plain why men would follow him, even into practically certain death—a master of men.

"I have another duty," he told the men quietly. "You can serve best by getting yourselves to safety, not wasting strength in purposeless battles. The revolt in Titustown failed. I go to save our people there."

He turned then, as precisely as a soldier, and marched off into the darkness. Silence followed him at first, then a ringing cheer. Nita's hand clasped his. Her hand was cold. It clung… clung, but there was no trembling there.

CHAPTER 2
CITY OF DOOM

TITUSTOWN WAS cupped in the hills, a rich valley that Dutch farmers had made fertile with their work. Industry had crept in and studded the banks of the broad, hurrying Carson River with factories. Now fifty thousand people lived there and from the crest of the surrounding hills, Titustown showed a neat pattern of corner street lights that extended for over a mile along the river and ran in precise lines up toward the piedmont slopes. Its glow reached up toward the black sky, borne on the smoke from a thousand chimneys, from homes.

It was doomed.

Around it, the Black Police had thrown a circle of steel. Every road that led from the valley was guarded, and the open fields, that stretched from outskirts to the down-reaching tongues of woodland, were commanded by machine guns and powerful searchlights. Across their prying beams patrols of armed men marched. Their shadows stretched, black and ominous, for hundreds of yards across the stricken land. Fugitives had been stopped. Some were flogged back toward the city, but most of them lay where they had been halted, by bullets.

Through the streets of Titustown rolled armored trucks in which patrols of Black Police quartered back and forth. Squads of men marched on foot, too, and where they moved cries of pain and terror arose. The whole city was being routed into the streets, crowded into central squares as the work of punishment went on.

One man in twenty-five would be shot. Of the remaining group, twelve would be marched into a concentration camp. Already, the first thin line of doomed people was filing out of the limits of the city toward the north. Their destination was fifty miles away. The night was cold and there were women and children mingled with the men. Already, some of them had felt the bite of the whips that drove on the laggards, or those who were too weak to keep the pace. Fifty miles like that....

Five miles away, a police roadster was roaring along the highway toward the city. A picket stopped it in the first gap of the hills and challenged the man in the uniform of the Black Police who drove it. The man's steely gray-blue eyes regarded the picket impassively, but a hand, below the side of the car, gripped an automatic.

"Password be damned," said the man in the car. "Your orders are to stop people coming out, not going in. I'm carrying messages."

The picket grinned. "You're right, at that," he said. "But don't think you can leave without the countersign."

The man in the car smiled thinly as he sent the machine

· *RICHARD WENTWORTH* ·

racing forward again. No, there would not be much trouble getting into the city of Titustown, but getting out would be a different matter. There was one countersign that opened all gates. The man touched his hand again to the automatic in his lap....

Then he went on.

In Titus Square, a still, huddled crowd of citizens had been herded together by the Black Police. There was a bandstand in its middle and it was against this that the men chosen to die were lined. Most of them were young; a few were brave. They stood unflinchingly before the lifting muzzles of the firing-squad. Others cowered on their knees and two were praying. The voices of the crowd were a babble of pleas, of indignation, of despair. Then the firing-squad officer's whistle piped, and he called *"Ready!"* Silence fell over the packed square—comparative silence. Somewhere, a child still whimpered and a man's pattering prayer lifted.

"Aim!"

Along the verge of the park rolled a police car with a single man behind the wheel, a hunch-shouldered man in a black cape. The car checked suddenly and, from its dark interior, the bright yellow flame of gunpowder lashed out! The firing-squad officer pitched against the nearest rifleman, but the gun continued to speak from the automobile, hammering death into that stiff line of executioners.

Even the whimpering of the child was stilled now, the silence unbroken save for those shattering gun blasts. There were other police on guard, but for seconds while those guns hammered, they were frozen, without comprehension.

Then a voice thundered from the car, *"Seize those rifles and fight! The Spider has come to save you!"*

Instantly, the police car with its sinister, black-caped driver leaped forward, whipped around a corner. The Black Police had awakened from their daze now and their guns began to speak, but the crowd had also snapped from the lethargy of terror. The men, a moment before certain of death, sprang to the weapons of the slain police.

"*The Spider!*" voices cried. "*The Spider has come!*"

It was a rallying cry. The prisoners no longer were passive under the threat of death and horror. Guns slammed, but the men who fired were pulled down and their weapons torn from them. Presently, sirens began to wail and motors roared heavily as reinforcements rushed to the scene.

A half block from the police headquarters, the Spider dropped the cape and was revealed once more in the black uniform of the tyrants. Reserves were rushing out. Truck loads of men in black uniforms were rolling toward Titus Square. The crashing of guns was continuous and the muttering roar of many voices, of a mob rocked by fierce anger, mingled with it.

The disguised Spider went bounding up the steps of police headquarters and into the hallway. "Where's the chief?" he demanded of the guard in the foyer.

The guard stared at him, gestured toward the steps. "What's happened?" he cried, but the Spider already was sprinting up the steps.

The building was ancient and the steps were wooden. The jail building was behind it and connected by a covered bridge. Another guard stood there, but to him the man in police uniform appeared a comrade. If he caught the steely glint of the gray-blue beneath the visor, it did not help to identify the man. How could he know that, racing toward him, was Richard Wentworth, the Spider!

Wentworth sent his voice vibrantly ahead of him. "Quick!" he snapped. "Into the jail! We've got to keep them locked in!"

The guard turned across the covered bridge, and Wentworth struck once swiftly as he overtook the man. He clanged shut the steel doors that separated the headquarters of the police from the jail, and raced on.

There were three men in the guardroom as Wentworth sprang inside. They were lounging about a table strewn with playing cards. Wentworth did not hesitate. He had, suddenly, a gun in each fist and he was striking with them before the men knew that he was attacking. He felled two men. The third skittered backward from the table, clawing for his gun. Wentworth swore, seized and flung a chair in the same movement, and went across the table in a long dive. The man's voice, lifted in a startled yell, broke short as the breath was driven from him. He crashed to the floor and Wentworth's swift-striking gun accounted for him also.

Wentworth heaved to his feet. His breath was coming in long, slow exhalations. His position was relaxed, ready, but his ears were tautly attuned. Had the sounds of his attack raised an alarm? No matter. There was no time for delay. The chances were it would be overlooked in the louder bedlam from outside. All the guards would be concentrating on that.

Wentworth bent over the unconscious men and swiftly thrust their guns into the waistband of his trousers. A coat hanging

on a wall peg had gold-laced chev-
rons on the sleeves. Swiftly, Went-
worth exchanged it for his own.
Then, deliberately, he strode into
the corridors beyond.

As in most old-fashioned jails,
the main hallway was closed by
two iron gratings and a man sat
usually at a desk between them.
Now, one of the gratings stood
open, and it was clear that the
guard was one of those Went-
worth already had struck down. He moved calmly through the
open grating and peered beyond.

THE JAIL was in darkness, but from it came the mutter of
many voices. Wentworth found a switch, closed it, and brilliant
light sprang up in the tiered cells beyond. Then he swore softly
under his breath. Every cell, made for two men, now contained
eight and ten. They were jammed in so that it was impossible
for anyone to lie down. Faces stared whitely at him between
the bars.

Without the loss of a moment, Wentworth snatched open
the locking lever of the cell doors, caught up the ring of keys and
dashed for the first cell. It was the work of an instant to unlock
it. He thrust the ring of keys at the first man to come out.

"Unlock all the cells," he ordered swiftly, then he sprang to a
central position where he could be seen from all tiers. Swiftly,

he whipped his silken cape from beneath his coat and flung it about his shoulders.

"Silence, men!" he called softly. "The Spider has come to rescue you!"

Despite his admonition, a muffled cheer went up, but it died quickly. Already, two more cells had been unlocked.

"I've created a diversion," he said, "I started a riot that has drawn most of the police from headquarters. If we are fast, well be able to seize their entire arsenal! Kirkpatrick, are you here?"

"Right above you, Dick!"

Wentworth peered upward, saw for the first time a cage of steel bars suspended near the ceiling. It was too small either to lie in or sit down, and Kirkpatrick's gaunt height was painfully contorted in his narrow prison. A cry burst from Wentworth's lips. His eyes swiftly followed the rope that suspended his friend and, in moments, he had freed him. Kirkpatrick reeled, braced himself against the torture cage.

"I knew you'd come, Dick," he said quietly. "What are the orders?"

With fumbling hands, he began to set his clothing in order and, irresistibly, a smile tugged at Wentworth's mouth corners. Even in this tense moment, Kirkpatrick would think of his appearance! His usually dapper clothing was ruined. But there was no time for pleasantries. Wentworth thrust the captured guns into his hands.

"Seize arms, Kirk," Wentworth snapped. "Take as many men as you can gather and rush to Titus Square. I started a riot there and if you make a flank attack on the Black Police, I think we'll have the bulk of their force within the city trapped. I'll follow as soon as the rest are freed!"

Kirkpatrick looked swiftly about him while he still exercised his gaunt body to restore the circulation of blood after his long, cramped confinement. His voice had the old crispness as he called out names and orders briskly. These were men Kirkpatrick knew. He had organized them for revolt and there was no hesitancy, no delay in the swift obedience to orders. A dozen men followed him.

While Wentworth made a swift estimate of the cells, he whipped a small packet from a pocket of the cape and hung a metal mirror on the bars of a cell. The light from overhead was brilliant, and he set deftly to work. He brushed his cheeks with liquid from a vial and the skin sallowed, drew taut across the bones. His lips vanished and his mouth became a sinister gash. It was the work of seconds then to change, with putty, his chiseled nose into a hawk-like, predatory beak. Thick bushy eyebrows covered his own and a lank, black wig hung about his nape. He drew on a black slouch hat, and, under the cape, his shoulders assumed a hunched and ominous aspect. In those few moments, the Spider had sprung alive again.

Wentworth turned to find men staring at him with wide, half-frightened eyes. He sent the flat, mocking laughter of the Spider at them, abruptly switched to his normal tone of voice.

"You'd almost think I was the Spider, wouldn't you," he laughed. "It will give the people courage to think they are led by the Spider. For you it will be enough to know it is your commander!"

The cheer of the men was spontaneous. There was burning enthusiasm in their eyes, a determination that he knew would carry them successfully against terrific odds. He had fully three hundred men. If he could arm them… Wentworth dispatched another squad to follow Kirkpatrick and to hold the arsenal when Kirkpatrick left to reinforce the fighting citizens.

"Hurry with unlocking those cells," Wentworth ordered. "We must be out of here in three minutes! Men, form in a column of squads here, quickly. Move slowly out through those gateways, but don't cross the bridge until we're all ready! I'm going ahead! Keep your ranks. We can move more swiftly that way when the time comes!"

Wentworth raced along the corridor. From ahead, a gun blasted out three times, then was silent. Wentworth tugged open the steel door that closed the bridge, then breathed deeply with relief. A half dozen of the Black Police were lined up against the wall under the guns of two of the liberated prisoners. One of the police lay dead upon the floor and, from the police arsenal, a line of grim rebels already was filing out. Kirkpatrick stood by the street door.

"Hurry, men!" Kirkpatrick barked. "At the double! Your families are fighting the Black Police for you!"

His squad tumbled down the steps, armed with rifles and revolvers. It was ten minutes before Wentworth's heavier column could form in the street in front of headquarters and follow. As they swung along at double time, the rapid crepitation of the battle in Titus Square came back to Wentworth. He flung a glance along the line of men. They seemed well disciplined. Kirkpatrick had done a good job. Wentworth checked while the column filed past and flung swift instructions in a low voice, raced back to his position at their head.

In an incredibly short time, the floodlights of Titus Square showed ahead. Instantly, Wentworth flung the column, divided, both ways from the corner. They spread out, paused.

"Charge!" Wentworth shouted. *"Death to the Black Police! The Spider leads you!"*

Wentworth's swift eye had spotted the scattered line of the police, ringing the square. Kirkpatrick had attacked at a point two blocks away, and already the mob of penned prisoners was streaming out through the breach he had made. At Wentworth's attack, there were a few scattered shots, then the Black Police broke and ran.

"Marksmen!" Wentworth called sharply. "Pick them off!"

The rout was complete, a skirmish had been won, but the main battle remained ahead. Wentworth sprang upon an abandoned police truck and sent his voice reaching across the multitude.

"All armed men to me!" he cried.

FIVE MINUTES later, he had started the column of jubilant people marching toward the city's edge under guard of a third of his augmented force. Their orders were to halt short of the machine-gun barricades which Wentworth knew were laid in ambush.

Rapidly he outlined his plans. Groups of the armed men were sent racing over the city in captured automobiles with orders to attack the Black Police wherever found; refugees were to be sent toward the exit of the city that Wentworth had chosen— the road by which he had entered. In that direction, within a dozen miles, lay the sanctuary of the hills. The people could not remain in their city, for, after this revolt, the Black Police would strike with the ruthlessness of which they were so fearfully capable. Artillery, airplane bombs… Only in flight, in scattering the people was there any safety.

With himself, Wentworth kept a group of ten men. At his orders, they swiftly stripped police uniforms from the bodies of the dead. Mounted on an armored truck then, they sped past the straggling column of refugees. Theirs was the task of opening the way. Kirkpatrick and Wentworth were wedged in beside the driver.

"I understand the necessity of flight, Dick," Kirkpatrick said slowly, his saturnine face more grave than usual, "but these multitudes will be found as easily in the hills as in a city. And how in the name of God will they be fed?"

Wentworth shook his head. "That's an impossibility," he said. "As soon as we have broken a way through, well go back to the city, seize every car we can find. As rapidly as the cars are loaded, the people will have to scatter over the state. The fighting men you have organized, we'll take into the hills. They will

be proscribed wherever they go. But the others won't be iden-
tifiable."

The driver said, quietly, "Picket just ahead, sir."

"Stop, when they challenge," Wentworth ordered. "Kirk, we'll
have to take out the sentries, and without noise if possible. We
have to pass two more before we're behind the machine-gun
barricades. After that, we can attack on their flanks—and the
road will be open!"

The sentry's challenge rang out, and, at Wentworth's order,
one of the uniformed men swung to the pavement as the truck
halted. "All right, sentry," he called. "I have a pass."

The man came toward the truck. When he was within reach,
Wentworth sprang. It was over in an instant—the man bound
and thrust out of sight in the roadside ditch. The truck rolled
on. The third sentry managed to get out a choked cry before he
was silenced, but apparently no alarm was given and, moments
later, Wentworth and Kirkpatrick led the silent file of men in a
flank attack upon the machine-gun emplacements. A single shot
was fired there, but the lack of discipline among the Black Police
prevented further trouble. Instead of investigating, near-by posts
of police contented themselves with shouted inquiries. Wentworth called back something about an accident, and they were
satisfied!

One by one, then, the other emplacements fell. There was a
pitched battle at the fourth, and Wentworth lost two men when
the operators managed to swing their machine-gun about. That
was the end. Wentworth left guards at the machine-guns, sent

for reinforcements and he and Kirkpatrick hurried back to the city to begin the work of scattering the refugees.

It was a frantic, heart-breaking task. Women wailed over leaving their homes; men were grim-faced and some were stubborn and slow to obey orders. There was, too, the ever-present danger that a column of Black Police might be on its way from some other point to quell the rebellion. Wentworth had tried to prevent an alarm from being sent out by severing communications but he could not be sure he had succeeded. Guards were thrown out to keep watch and, an hour after sun-up when the harassing job was finally completed, no enemy had been sighted. But with daylight their danger increased from airplane patrols!

The city was deserted now save for sulkers and the few who had flatly refused to leave. Wentworth's three hundred men had been augmented by another fifty—and there was no transportation for them. The city had been swept bare of motor vehicles of any kind. They could not delay their departure. It would be impossible to hold Titustown against any sizable attack with his worn-out men. They must take flight to the hills, twelve miles away, and the trip must be made on foot!

AFTER A hurried meal on canned goods, taken from an already looted store, the march got under way. Wentworth threw out men ahead of the column and on the flanks to guard against surprise attacks. Kirkpatrick and himself walked at the head of the line and set the pace. Despite the weariness of the night's labor, the men were jubilant. A heavy blow had been struck at the morale of the Black Police and families delivered from a savage vengeance. They marched behind leaders whom they admired and trusted. Some one started a low-voiced song and soon the whole column was singing:

"Oh, the Black Police, they think they're tough,
  Parley-vous.
The Black Police, they think they're rough,
  Parley-vous.
But when they found we wouldn't bluff,
They were glad, by God, to yell enough.
  Hinky-dinky, parley-vous!"

Kirkpatrick's grim face relaxed in a slight smile as he nodded to Wentworth, beside whom he marched. "They're in good spirits, right now," he said. "I'd stack them against three times their number of Black Police."

"We may have to," Wentworth told him flatly, and explained about the ambush and evacuation of the cavern hideaway.

"The devil!" Kirkpatrick muttered. "And the nearest camp, aside from that one, is a hundred miles or more! We're heading for the cavern anyway?"

"There's no choice," Wentworth said quietly. "There are supplies hidden there. It's just possible that our attack wiped out all the men who knew about it, but we won't work on that assumption." Abruptly, he stopped. Two shots from the advanced guard had sounded. He whirled toward his men. "Airplane coming!" he shouted. "Off the road and scatter! Lie flat!"

The song broke off short, and the men scattered into the fields and thin woods. Wentworth found himself prone beside Kirkpatrick while he lifted field-glasses to scan the skies to west-

31

ward. The roar of the airplane engine came rapidly nearer and Wentworth finally brought it in focus.

"Police machine all right," he said quietly.

It swept over and on toward Titustown, slanted down to a landing. Wentworth piped shrilly on a police whistle, and the men quickly formed into a column again, went at double-time up the slow grade toward the surrounding hills. When the plane took the air again, the men had reached the cover of the woods near the ridges, but Wentworth's forehead was set in a frown.

"That means trouble all the way to the hills," he said quietly. "Perhaps a fight when we get there. Kirk, we'll never put an end to those devils in Albany and New York by any such tactics as this."

Kirkpatrick agreed moodily. The men were no longer singing. They needed breath for marching, and Wentworth set them a hard pace. Once an hour, they would rest for ten minutes, then swing on. There was need for haste, because open country lay between them and the sanctuary of the hills. There was a single town on their path, two miles ahead. If they could reach that....

"Dick, you have no new theories as to the identity of the man behind all this—the Master, the Face in the Mirror*—whatever you want to call him?"

---

* AUTHOR'S NOTE: The Master's secret, organized behind the criminal elements that ruled the state, apparently was unknown even to his lieutenants. It was quite plain that the man was clever in the line of physics. For example, in the office of Governor Whiting, there was a curious concave mirror. When certain words were spoken a white face appeared, and it was

Wentworth shook his head briefly, and there was a hard glint in his gray-blue eyes. "It's only clear that he must be some one who has easy access to the Governor and the Mayor of New York.

"That face in the mirror is an obvious trick, but it makes it necessary for him to be at that spot occasionally. Some of his messages are undoubtedly phonographic. He's clever at disguise, too, apparently. For a time, he posed as Whiting's secretary, and I'm convinced not even Whiting knew the man was really the Master. When we tracked him down in that disguise, he simply discarded it and fled."*

"Then you have no new evidence?" Kirkpatrick's voice was heavy. "You were going to Albany…."

"I found out nothing there that might point to the Master," Wentworth said, "but I think I have devised a way in which we can kidnap Governor Whiting. If we could get him to one of our camps, we might be able to make him talk… if he knows anything. At least, we might force the Master out into the open. With Whiting gone, he might be compelled to take active control. That, at least, is what I'm hoping. But first this column must be placed in safety, and…."

Once more, from the advance guard came the two shots which signaled the approach of an airplane and Wentworth

in this way the Master gave his orders. From this, also, he was known as the White Face in the Mirror.

* AUTHOR'S NOTE: The details of this attempt were told in that adventure of the Spider called "The City That Paid to Die."

shouted his orders. There was no cover this time, only the open fields to each side.

"They'll be looking for us this trip," Wentworth said quietly to Kirkpatrick. "That town is still a mile ahead. If we can reach that, we'll commandeer automobiles."

The plane droned rapidly nearer and swung in a wide circle over the scattered column of men. Wentworth swore under his breath, lifted his voice.

"Two squads of men to me!" he called sharply, and indicated the men he wanted. When they were close about him, he organized them into a compact group, kneeling, rifles at ready.

"At my order," he said quietly, "we will fire a volley. Lead the plane by two yards. The idea is to throw up a wall of lead into which he will dive. We'll fire as a squad—ready, aim, and *fire*. Understood?" He turned to Kirkpatrick. "It would be much more effective with the entire company, but there isn't time to organize them, and...."

"I'll form a squad across the road," Kirkpatrick said quickly, and darted to the other side of the highway.

THE PLANE was swinging lower now and a dark speck plummeted down from beneath it... a bomb! Wentworth followed its course with narrow eyes, but it struck wide. The concussion rolled across the fields. A second bomb followed, but it was also wide. A taut smile moved Wentworth's lips. The plane would come lower now, to make sure of its target and, when it did....

"Kirk!" he called softly. "Have your men fire at my command also!"

His call was just in time. The pilot of the plane, encouraged by the lack of resistance, swung in a wide bank and dived down over the road. A bomb rocketed downward, striking the concrete two hundred yards away. The concussion was shattering, and fragments of metal and stone whined

hoarsely through the air. A man screamed on a rising pitch, was still.

"Ready!" Wentworth called steadily. "Aim…."

The plane was roaring toward them. Its machine guns began to hammer, and above its chattering and the heavy thunder of the engine, Wentworth's voice rang out clearly.

"Fire!"

The combined blast of the rifles beat down the plane's racket, and Wentworth called out again, sped a second volley at the ship. There was a ragged cheer from the men as the plane wavered, zoomed in a steep climb. Two hundred, three hundred feet it soared until it seemed virtually to hang on its propeller. Then it slid off in a stall. An instant later, it struck the earth and its remaining bombs exploded together. The plane was torn to bits. Fragments of it were hurled high into the air.

Everywhere, Wentworth's men were on their feet, cheering madly. But there was no time for delay. Wentworth's whistle shrilled imperatively, and he sent the column at double-time toward the village. He stood watching them hurry past and, abruptly, a worried light appeared in his eyes. Most of the men ran well, with cheerful faces, but there were others who staggered in their pace. Their eyes were dull and their heads swung. One stumbled and pitched heavily to his face, and it was a long moment before he began to push himself to his feet.

Wentworth hurried to his side, helped him up. The man's eyes were bright with fever, but there was a carious, almost lustrous whiteness to his skin. He held his gun against his side by the pressure of his forearm and his hands were claw-like.

"What's the matter?' Wentworth asked quietly. "Are you sick?"

The man's face twitched. "Sick, yes," he said thickly. "It's got me—the White Face sickness."

"Nonsense, man!" Wentworth said sharply. "What are you talking about?"

The man threw back his head and his voice came out hoarsely, with obvious effort. "It gets you if you fight the Black Police. They warned us, and…" His gun slipped out from under his arm. "My arms are going dead, too. No feeling in my hands or feet."

He held his clawed hand up before him, struck his fists together violently. The end joint of one of his fingers broke off, but there was no blood, and apparently he felt no pain. He stared at it, and screaming laughter began to pump from his lips. He tore from Wentworth's grip and began to run wildly across the field!

The tail of the column had passed now, but Wentworth was aware of faces twisted about, staring palely back. The sick man had fallen again and seemed unable to push himself off the ground. Wentworth ran to him, saw the man struggling toward his knees. Even as Wentworth reached him, it was too late. With a convulsive effort, the man had driven a knife into his breast!

Horror shook Wentworth, and his mind flashed back to the warning Nita had given him long ago… God, it was only last night! *"Some horrible new disease, like leprosy…."*

A shudder racked Wentworth, but he could not stay here. The column was already three hundred yards away. He could help the dead man no longer. He swung about and began to lope steadily after the men. The village was drawing closer, but he would have to rest the column first. This sickness was a new and insidious complication.

If that thought, which the sick man had voiced—that the White Face sickness attacked those who fought the Black Police—was widely circulated, it would utterly subdue the people of the state. Here was an end of all revolt… Wentworth swore bitterly. *If* it were circulated? The Black Police would strew the state with propaganda! Here was a weapon more powerful than any armed force. The Master was clever!

WENTWORTH HALTED the column for two minutes to rest. While the panting men flung themselves down, he moved swiftly along the line and, as inconspicuously as possible, inspected their condition. As he moved, his horror increased. Fully a dozen of them showed the symptoms of the White Face disease! They were not as well marked as in the man who had died. One was stamping his feet as if they were numb; another was curiously working his fingers. In the eyes of all of them was that curious fever brightness accompanied by a contrasting pallor of their cheeks.

The Black Police had arrived and turned
the rocky fortress into a giant gallows.

"Fall out," Wentworth ordered them curtly, and added, with a brief smile, "We must throw out a rear guard to watch against pursuit from Titustown."

He could not afford to have panic spread through the line, nor could he risk contagion. In this way, he could isolate the men

and, being behind the column, their ultimate collapse would not spread panic. He had no intention of abandoning the men. Once they reached camp, he must devise some treatment. There were injections which would cure leprosy in its early stages… *chaulmoogra* oil.

Wentworth hurried on to the head of the column. They were now close to the environs of the city and could slow their pace a little. Once they acquired automobiles… Toward them, along the road, a car was speeding. As Wentworth reached Kirkpatrick's side, the machine halted and a man hurried toward them. Fright was in his face.

"We have to ask you to detour around the town," the man said.

Wentworth regarded the man impassively.

This was a new development. He had found most people eager to help him against the Black Police. They had regarded Wentworth and his men as their protectors. But now….

The man hurried on. "I'm sorry, sir, but that's the way it is. You have the White Face plague in your blood. You're bound to! You've been fighting the Black Police."

Wentworth stared at the man incredulously. So that damnable propaganda already was at work! God, the Master fought with shrewd weapons! There might be some slight danger of contagion, but he could hold his men together in the village and push on rapidly. They had to enter, to obtain transportation and food. Without these necessities, his whole column would be doomed. Even as he confronted the man, Wentworth heard once more the signal shots of his lookouts which meant another airplane, perhaps a group of them, was headed this way!

"You are mad, man!" Wentworth said sharply. "No one in your town will be harmed." He lifted his voice. "Forward… *march!*"

The column swung on, and the townsman leaped from the road. "I've warned you!" he cried violently. "We're not going to have the White Face plague in our town! Every man in there is ready for you with guns. That tree—" he pointed to a twisted oak no more than a hundred yards ahead of the column—"that oak tree is the deadline. The minute your men pass that point, *we open fire!*"

CHAPTER 3
CAMP DESPAIR

WENTWORTH CONFRONTED the man who wore a sheriff's badge on his coat, and cold anger surged through him. Were they to be stopped by this man's stupidity when safety was so close? But he could not order his men to fight against the citizens of the town. It was to defend such as these that he had taken the field of battle against the Black Police and their white-faced Master. Now, the people for whom he fought were opposing him… He threw a quick glance at the skies. There were three airplanes this time. The column had almost reached the tree….

Wentworth blew a shrill blast on his whistle. "Two files to

each side of the road—as skirmishers. But wait for the order to open fire!"

He turned to the sheriff. "My troops could crush your two-penny defense in a few minutes," he said patiently, "but I prefer to avert bloodshed."

The sheriff was white-faced, shaken. He had anticipated no such hostile answer to his challenge. Wentworth's friendship, his desire to help the people was too well known. The man wet his lips with a furtive tongue.

"Really, sir," he said hoarsely. "You do not wish to infect us with the plague."

"That is arrant nonsense!" Wentworth told him sharply, "but I will humor you on one condition. You will either lend me fifteen large trucks or four times that number of automobiles, or we will march into town and take them. It is for you to say!" Wentworth lifted his voice. "Kirkpatrick! Try some volleys at those planes!"

The ships were swooping very close now. Wentworth turned imperturbably back to the sheriff. "Well, which will it be, man?" he demanded. "Will you bring out the trucks and cars at once—or shall we take them?"

A volley crashed out, was echoed by the heavy blast of a bomb. The sheriff trembled, glanced over his shoulder. A dozen of his armed men were running frantically back along the street, away from the scene of battle.

"You shall have the trucks and cars at once," he whispered. "They'll be returned, I hope, sir?"

"Report them stolen," Wentworth said carelessly. "No doubt,

your friends, the Black Police, will return them to you. Now, hurry! I'll give you five minutes to get the machines here. Your own will do for a starter!"

Another airplane bomb burst nearer at hand, and fragments of metal whined overhead. The concussion sucked at Wentworth's clothing. The sheriff turned and ran back toward the town. He was fat and fled awkwardly. He kept glancing up at the swooping planes.

The three were diving in formation now, and Kirkpatrick had the entire company organized, ready to fire upward. Wentworth saw his arm raised, the whistle between his lips. A bomb burst at the far end of the ragged line of skirmishers and two men were blown, tumbling, through the air. Then the whistle skirled, the guns crashed together. The leading plane wavered and slid off to the right, recovered. Its engine began to miss fire and black smoke belched from under the motor cowling. Another ship was towering like a wounded bird. A second volley crashed out, but the third plane slanted low and went, hedge-hopping, at frantic speed toward the cover of the hills.

The men were cheering again. Flames had followed the gout of smoke from the cowling of the first ship. Its pilot sprang overside, but he was too close to the ground and struck before his 'chute could open. The second ship was spinning, out of control, toward the earth. A geyser of earth blasted upward when it struck with its load of bombs.

"Hold your line, Kirk!" Wentworth called. "We're having a bit of trouble with these villagers."

Even as he spoke, a first automobile was rolling out of the

town. Its driver parked it on the road, took one glance toward Wentworth and ran heavily back toward the protection of the buildings. Wentworth moved toward Kirkpatrick.

"We can't look for any more luck like that," Kirkpatrick said quietly. "After that escaping plane has given warning, they'll fly high and drop their bombs from a distance. The Black Police will probably send a motorized car after us."

Wentworth nodded and repeated his conversation with the sheriff.

"What the hell did he mean—White Face plague?" Kirkpatrick asked sharply. When he had heard of the infected men within the ranks of the company, his face became stern and sharply lined. "We have no weapons against such callous slaughter as that," he said harshly. "If the people turn against us, too… We'd better get some of the men started, don't you think?"

"I'm not sure the sheriff will perform, if we weaken our threat of invasion," Wentworth told him wearily. "I'm afraid we'll have to wait. Send messengers to call in the flankers and the rear guard, if any of the latter are left alive. It looks like leprosy, Kirk. We'll have to send a raiding party to one of the New York laboratories and try to get hold of chalmoogra oil for injections."

"We can thank the Master for this!" Kirkpatrick said violently. "By God, if I could get my hands on him, I'd strangle him!"

Wentworth smiled faintly. "Without due process of law, Kirk?"

Kirkpatrick's face remained grim. "This is once when the Spider's methods would be justified! Why not throw aside pretense, Dick, and appear in your own right as the Spider? It would hearten the men. It's all right for you to say you're only using the Spider's seal and identity because it will help terrify your enemies. But the other role would be stronger."

"No doubt it would," Wentworth agreed quietly. "I wish the Spider would join forces with us."

KIRKPATRICK TURNED impatiently away to the men. Kirkpatrick had long been convinced that Wentworth was the Spider, but there could be no confession. Some day, Wentworth hoped to reinstate his friend as Commissioner of New York Police. He was invaluable in his service to the people that way. If he knew that Wentworth was the Spider... Wentworth shook his head. No, the present method would have to serve. Frankly assuming the Spider's identity would not increase his men's loyalty. He had told them only that the Spider was his friend—that he had the right to use the seal and he had given to a few of them that right also. It was a potent weapon against the Black Police....

It was a half hour before Wentworth could finally load his men into the assembled automobiles and push on through the town toward the retreat in the hills. This way, the retreat would take no more than half an hour... When the motorcade neared the spot at which he had been ambushed, Wentworth halted and sent men ahead on foot. The barricade had been swept away. Hope sprang up in his heart.

At top speed, he pushed on toward the hidden woods lane that led to the camp. When he reached it, fear began to run coldly through his veins. The bushes were trampled and beaten down and there were the tire marks of many cars. Surely, Sailor

Joe and Nita would not have been as careless as that, even though they were abandoning the camp. Both had known that the evacuation was only precautionary.

He could see from the stiffening of Kirkpatrick's body that the same thought had flashed into his mind. If there had been a raid, and the Black Police were still here... Swiftly, Wentworth got the men out of their cars and organized them into a thin column. Rapidly, he surveyed them and despair ran through him. Once more, he saw the tell-tale symptoms of the plague. Men stumbled in their stride, or fumbled their guns with numb fingers, and the fever was in their eyes—ten, fifteen, a score of his diminishing force. But it would be useless now to separate them from the others. He strode to the fore of his line of men and led the way cautiously on through the woods, across the fields beyond and over the creek.

The way rose sharply from that point and heavy glacial boulders made a natural fortress about the cavern's mouth. But it was not the frowning menace of the trap that might have been set among them that brought Wentworth to a sharp, incredulous halt. A score of bodies dangled limply against the face of those rocks, the bodies of dead men. No need to guess what had happened. The Black Police had arrived in force before the cavern could be evacuated—and had turned that rocky fortress' face into a giant gallows tree! Such defenders as had been captured alive had been hanged out of hand by the ruthless forces of the Master!

With a frantic cry rising in his throat, Wentworth started to hurl himself forward... and didn't. Those murders might

well be bait for a trap, to
induce whatever force
came to dash in unwarily.
His voice shaken with fury,
Wentworth ordered men to
climb to points of vantage
and reconnoiter. It was only
when they had reported the

way was clear that Wentworth pushed on.

THE SCENE inside the barrier was appalling with its proof
of cruelty. Men and women had been tortured here. Their piti-
ful bodies still bore the marks of fiery torment, and the cavern
itself was a shambles. His face rigid as stone, Wentworth made
himself move slowly about his quest, for Nita van Sloan had
been here. They would be sure to single her out… He stopped
abruptly as he caught the faint signs of life in one of the tortured
victims. He knelt beside the man whose eyelids had fluttered.

"Torture," the man whispered. "Water!"

Wentworth gave him whisky from a flask, and the man
revived a little—and with it came renewal of his pain. His limbs
were crushed and horribly twisted beneath him. His hands…
Wentworth fought down the strong shudder that tugged at his
nerves.

"Miss van Sloan… prisoner," the man whispered. "Sailor
Joe… Albany."

"Taken to Albany?" Wentworth snapped.

The man nodded feebly. "Tortured them there… information. I… I had to live until…" His body jerked and, with a final gasping breath, the life went out of him.

Wentworth rose stiffly to his feet and peered around once more. His force of men stood in dejected, exhausted attitudes. They had fought through a long night, marched rapidly for miles—only to find death and slaughter at the end. The plague… Wentworth's eyes sharpened as he glanced over the wavering line of men. God! *Fully half of them were stricken with the White Face horror!*

Even while he stood watching them, one of the men let fall his gun and stared, with bulging eyes, at his clawed hands. A hoarse scream tore from his throat.

"My hands!" he cried. "My hands. I…I can't feel them!"

Wentworth sprang forward. "You're sick," he said. "Lie down there in the shade. All of you rest. Well arrange for food and medicine. *At once!*"

The man who had screamed was staring at him piteously. "God!" he whispered. "Its true! We fought the Black Police and… and we've got the plague!"

"Silence!" Wentworth snapped. "If you are ill, it is because some one had fed you germs or injected a virus into your veins. It has nothing to do with fighting the police!"

The man subsided, lay down in the shade as Wentworth had ordered, but it was plain that the fear which had brushed him laid its cold hand upon the rest. Wentworth stepped to Kirkpatrick's side.

"I think most of our force is infected," he said softly. "There's only one thing to do. We'll have to send a raiding party to seize supplies from some hospital. Albany will be our best bet. If we can't get any action, we'll have to capture some of the Black Police and… question them!"

Kirkpatrick nodded stiffly. "I'll stay here and do what I can for them, Dick," he said. "You go to Albany. And for God's sake, get Nita out of those madmens' hands!"

Wentworth's face was drawn and pale. He could not allow himself to think of Nita in the hands of the Black Police, but he must. His inclination was to send Kirkpatrick on that errand, to remain here where the peril of the plague was greatest… but Kirkpatrick was right. Wentworth was more skillful in such raids.

Wentworth nodded curtly. "Very well, Kirk. You still have about a hundred effectives here. I'm going on alone. No, it's better that way! We have a few allies in Albany. I'll go to them, or else to the Catskill camp. If I took men with me, they might only… spread the plague!"

Kirkpatrick nodded, held out his hand. The two men shook hands with a strong clasp, but neither of them spoke the things that were in their hearts. Each knew that they might never meet again, that death would be lying in wait at every turn of the road. And the power of the Black Police was waxing hourly. The stroke of loosing this plague, with its propaganda, would rob Wentworth's pitifully small band of every ally. The attack on the cavern had destroyed a third of his men. There were only two other camps—the main one in the Catskills, another hidden nearer New York City in the vicinity of Peekskill and if they….

Abruptly, Wentworth whipped about at a startled cry behind

him. A man he recognized as a messenger from the Catskill camp had just entered the fortress. He came rapidly forward.

"Commander," he said hurriedly in an undertone. "Jackson, commanding at Catskill, sent me with news. Jackson has sent out another man to try to get your message through to Washington. The first one was caught and… hanged."

"Surely," Kirkpatrick put in, "Washington doesn't need a message from you to know what is going on here!"

Wentworth shook his head. His voice came out dully. "Everything is legal on the surface, Kirk," he said. "Washington won't know of such things as happened here. If they found out, we would be classed as armed rebels against the government. Things were almost as bad as this in the South, you remember, until an assassin managed to shoot the dictator there. And the government could do nothing. They'll step in fast enough, if there is basis, but until they have the evidence… If this second messenger fails, I'll go myself!"

"There's more news, sir," the messenger hurried on. "The state has been put under quarantine because of the plague. The border guards have been strengthened!"

Wentworth nodded again in acknowledgment. "Kirk, I'll send back medical supplies at the first possible moment." While he spoke he was rapidly stripping off the Spider disguise and once more was a Black Police official. He turned to the messenger. "Your name?"

"Perrin, sir," the man saluted. He was a chubby, cheerful man.

"Very well, Perrin. Come with me."

THE MEN raised a ragged cheer as Wentworth went out

through the narrow entrance to the fortress, but it was pitifully weak. It hurt something inside of Wentworth. As long as men could cheer, there was perhaps some hope. Perhaps....

When Wentworth reached the line of cars in which they had fled, men sent by Kirkpatrick already were hurrying after him to drive them to the encampment. Wentworth entered a small, swift car, and Perrin slid in quickly behind the wheel.

"Where to, sir?" he asked cheerfully.

"Albany," Wentworth ordered quietly.

"It's under martial law, sir!" Perrin urged. "I had to skirt it when I came up here."

Wentworth's lips tightened in grimness, but there was no help for the course he must follow. "Very well," he agreed. "Stop five miles short of Albany, and we'll lay plans. I'm going to catch a nap. Wake me, then."

Wentworth relaxed against the cushions then, forced his eyes to close—drove despair, all thoughts, from his mind. It took an enormous concentration of will to accomplish that, for his tired brain raced with fears and conjectures. He was realizing now that it had been more than twenty-four hours since he had slept or rested. Weariness swept over him like a weakening fever. He slept... It was this remarkable ability to force sleep upon himself at need that enabled Wentworth to keep going long after most other men would have succumbed to fatigue. He awoke presently at Perrin's touch on his arm, instantly in full possession of his senses and enormously refreshed. He glanced sharply around him.

The sun was slanting toward the west and there was a chill on the November air which meant the night would be cold. The car was parked beside a narrow asphalt road that wound through trees ahead. Beyond the crest of the next hill, Wentworth could see the smoke smudge of a city against the sky.

"Albany?" he asked quietly.

Perrin assented, "Have you any orders, sir?"

"None as yet," Wentworth replied quietly. "Military law was established after I left Albany yesterday. Do you have an idea how stringent it is?"

"The word is, sir, that it was set up to prevent spread of the plague."

The plague was damnably convenient! It gave the state government excuse for the most rigid measures of control—and it would account for any deaths that the Black Police might wish to inflict secretly or in their concentration camps. Also it would make neighboring states anxious to assist them in preventing anyone's escape across the border. Yes, the plague was convenient as more than a weapon of propaganda and subjugation! To Wentworth, it was inconceivable, however, that so shrewd a man as the Master would release wholesale contagion upon the state—unless he possessed the means of controlling it!

Either the White-Face plague was not contagious at all, but was spread by germs being fed or injected into the veins of the intended victims—all the victims had come from the group who had been in jail—or all of the Black Police had been rendered immune by injections. There must be an anti-toxin if this were not a true leprosy, or else large quantities of the chaulmoogra oil specific, and surely Albany would have a supply… Thus Wentworth drove himself first of all to the errand of mercy he must perform for those brave men he had left stricken behind him. All his soul cried out that he strike immediately to free those who were being tortured for information, Nita and the rest. But....

"Our headquarters first," Wentworth directed. "Drive openly into the city. This uniform of the Black Police should still serve to get me past the guards. I've commandeered your car."

Perrin nodded, though his full face for once was grave, and sent the car speeding ahead. Presently, he swung out into a main highway. Wentworth was apprehensive over the guard, but they passed him quickly. They were not the Black Police, but men of the National Guard in khaki uniforms, and Wentworth swore under his breath as Perrin wove the car dexterously through Albany streets. If soldiers had displaced the Black Police in Albany, it would make his task doubly difficult. He had no scruples about using firearms against the tyrant and criminal police, but against these men his guns were holster-bound. The Spider did not harm the innocent!

ONLY TWO of his men were present in the Albany spy headquarters, a small side-street restaurant, when Wentworth entered there, but they gave him valuable information. The Black Police still stood guard over the governor's offices and home, but the rest of the city was under control of the troops under Colonel Roscoe Rice.

"Colonel Rice!" Wentworth exclaimed softly. "In God's name, what can a man of Rice's quality be doing as the ally of these crooks!"

The man in charge of the restaurant, an oldish former army

man named Brace, laughed shortly. "The odor of sanctity, sir!" he told Wentworth. "They are getting a little worried about Washington after catching your messenger."

In the back room of the restaurant, Wentworth paced the floor for a few minutes in deep concentration. "This may be a fortunate break for us," he said finally. "These are the orders. Two men to the hospital to seize supplies of anti-toxin or whatever injections they employ, by any means possible and rush it to the Cavern. The rest of you, with Perrin to help, will seize a group of officials. Brace, you'll know the ones to select, which will be easy to find and capture. They must be men allied to the Master and the Black Police. Blindfold them and take them to the Catskill camp. If my efforts fail, we'll use them as hostages for the safe return of our companions who are being held by the police. Understood?"

Brace nodded briskly, "Of course, sir. And you? You'll go directly to the camp, won't you, sir? This town is dangerous for you. A great many of the men stationed here know you by sight. We can't afford to have anything happen to you, commander."

Wentworth smiled and clapped a hand on Brace's bowed, but still sturdy shoulder. "What I'm going to do," he said, "is a job I couldn't assign to any one else. I'm calling on Colonel Rice! I'm going to persuade him to desert the Master, enlist under me and turn over all his prisoners."

In spite of Brace's army training, his jaw sagged at that announcement, but Wentworth cut him short; set him to work to gather all his men and begin the raids at once. Wentworth sprang to the steps that led to the living quarters above and there rapidly threw off the garb of the Black Police.

When, a few moments later, he hurried to the street, he was completely in his own identity. He wore the neat dark tweeds of which he was so fond and a light topcoat, a soft brown felt drawn low upon his black brows. He was taking his life in his hands, but the soldier guards were not apt to recognize him. Colonel Rice would, for Wentworth knew him personally. That was in accordance with his plans!

DUSK WAS blue in the city streets when Wentworth made his way toward the armory headquarters and there was a refreshing briskness in the air. The day after Thanksgiving… The thought was ironic. There was little for which the people of New York State could be grateful! The fact that they were alive, perhaps, but even that was a mixed blessing….

At the entrance of the armory, a sentry challenged Wentworth.

"I bring an official message," Wentworth told him curtly. "Take me at once to Colonel Rice."

The crisp authority of his voice accomplished more than his words, and he was passed rapidly to the sergeant of the guard, then to the anteroom of Colonel Rice. His adjutant was a man Wentworth did not know, but he wasted no time with him, insisted that his message was for Colonel Rice alone. When the adjutant rose to show him to the inner office, Wentworth stepped close and struck with a chopping punch of his right fist behind the ear. It was not the method he would have chosen, but there was no help for it. Colonel Rice would recognize him instantly and might very well order his arrest before he had a chance to talk at all. Rapidly strapping the adjutant's wrists with his own belt, Wentworth heaved the man to his shoulder, opened the door of the inner office and walked in. He had an automatic in his fist.

"I'll trouble you not to call the guard, Colonel Rice!" he said crisply.

Behind his desk, Colonel Rice sprang to his feet. He had a fighter's jaw, and his eyes were cold and arbitrary beneath bushy iron-gray brows.

"What the hell do you mean? Adjutant!"

Wentworth deposited the adjutant on the floor and moved quickly to the desk, removing his hat. Colonel Rice stared at him.

"Wentworth!" he rasped. "Major Wentworth! What does this conduct mean? Damn it, man, there are a dozen warrants out for your arrest! I'll have you in irons…."

Wentworth thrust his automatic into the holster. Colonel Rice had not called the guard. He didn't think the officer would until he had opportunity to speak. If he did….

"I came to ask you a question, Colonel," be said shortly. "How long have you been taking orders from murderers and thieves?"

Colonel Rice's jaw dropped, then angry blood surged into his throat. "What the hell do you mean?"

Wentworth leaned across the desk. "Don't you realize, Rice," he demanded, "that the state government is in the hands of criminals? Governor Whiting is no more than a puppet who jumps at the orders of a crook. But you take orders from him!

You police this city for him! You hold prisoners who are being tortured at this moment. Tortured, sir! One of them is my fiancée, Nita van Sloan. I think you know her, Rice."

"You're mad!" Rice sank heavily into his seat. "Torturing… Miss van Sloan?"

"You haven't answered my question," Wentworth pointed out sharply. "Don't you realize you are being used as a tool by criminals?"

Colonel Rice's short-cut hair bristled. "Confound you, Wentworth," he said, "don't be a fool! I'm a soldier! When the governor issues orders, I obey!"

Wentworth smiled faintly. "When the Federal government takes over here, I'm afraid they won't recognize your innocence, Colonel Rice. They're apt to hang you as high as Governor Whiting."

Rice sat still through a silent moment, but in those few seconds, a subtle change crept over his face. It was no longer belligerent and angry. It was suddenly very tired.

"You knew all that," Wentworth said quietly, "and you don't approve, Colonel Rice. That was why you didn't order me arrested the moment I came in here. There's an incomparable opportunity here for you. Muster your men and declare Governor Whiting for what he is—a criminal! You could seize the government and, in a few days, we would cleanse this state of all the criminals who rule it now!"

Colonel Rice stared at him incredulously. "Armed rebellion against the state?" he gasped. "Damn it, sir, that's mutiny! Whiting was legally elected. He's my commanding officer!"

"Not at all," Wentworth said quietly. "Governor Whiting is betraying the people who elected him. Even if he is your superior officer, he is subject to arrest by you as a traitor! The people would support you overwhelmingly! Damn it, Whiting has released this plague on the people who oppose him!"

Colonel Rice shook his head. "It sounds splendid," he said. His anger was gone now, but he was quiet, assured. "What you don't realize is that I am absolutely helpless. I am surrounded by spies. No doubt your arrival is already being reported to the Black Police. And I don't have a regiment here, only two companies of comparatively undisciplined and unskilled men—no machine guns. The Black Police are in force all about the governor and the capitol, and fully prepared for any such attack. It would be just about hopeless."

"But you'll permit me to take away those prisoners?" Wentworth urged. "Surely, you can't countenance torturer?"

"They shall not be tortured, if I can prevent it!" Colonel Rice assured him, "but I'm not at all sure I can prevent it. In precisely one minute, I'm going to call the guard and have you put under arrest, Wentworth. One minute." He shot his cuff and looked at his watch.

Wentworth drew a deep breath, "I hate to do this, Colonel Rice," he said, "but if you lift your voice, I'll shoot!"

The eyes of the two men met fiercely and there was no wavering in either. "You have thirty seconds left," Colonel Rice said flatly.

Wentworth laughed and holstered his automatic.

In a long stride, he reached the adjutant's side and whipped his sword from its sheath. "You have your sword," Colonel Rice he cried. *"Draw!* I'll fight you to see whether I surrender or you enlist under me for the duration of the war against Governor Whiting! But I warn you, the only way you can win is by cutting me down!"

For a moment longer, the eyes of the two men held, then Colonel Rice said shortly, "Done! I promise that if you surrender, you'll have a fair trial if it takes my entire two companies to guarantee it. If I lose, and am able, I'll send my resignation to the governor and go with you! After I resign, what you accomplish in the direction of freeing prisoners will rest on my subordinate."

Colonel Rice came lithely around the desk, his movements light and sure. He swung the saber hissing through the air, flexed his wrist. "I warn you," he said grimly, "I was fencing champion at West Point!"

Wentworth laughed again. "On guard, Colonel Rice! It will be a pleasure to have a man like you fighting from now on at my side!"

The sabers leveled, and the two men glided toward each other until the steel clashed lightly. Then Colonel Rice attacked with the sudden fury of an electric storm.

The fight began.

CHAPTER 4
FATE'S SWORDSMAN

WENTWORTH HAD a set plan in mind before their sabers clashed in the first slash and parry. He intended to disarm Colonel Rice and enlist him in the battle against the Master of the criminals. Besides the prestige his force would gain from the desertion, he would acquire a clever leader for armed men. Wentworth had no illusions about the future.

Not that an easy task lay ahead of him. Colonel Rice's saber was a darting, steel serpent and it was plain that he was in excellent condition, and practice. Adding to Wentworth's difficulty was the fact that he did not want to wound the colonel—and there was constant danger of interruption from other men. It was true the door was locked, yet....

Wentworth was forced to drive all divergent thoughts from his mind and concentrate on the saber duel. A fighting thrust with the edge had been averted only by an utterly unorthodox parry which threw Wentworth's saber completely out of line. Before Colonel Rice could take advantage of the fact, Wentworth leaped in so close that the sabers could not be brought to bear. When he sprang back again, he was on guard.

A grim smile moved Colonel Rice's lips. "Do you wish to surrender?" he demanded. "I have the honor of first blood."

It was not until he spoke that Wentworth realized the slight stinging burn in his cheek had come from the bite of his opponent's saber. The thrust had been even closer than he thought!

Wentworth laughed. "I warned you, Colonel he said lightly. "I won't surrender while I can still lift the saber!"

Colonel Rice was pressing his fancied advantage. His saber whirled in a powerful bead cut, spun and slashed at the legs. Wentworth sprang back and an oath of dismay forced itself out. He had forgotten the adjutant might have recovered consciousness. As he leaped, the adjutant struck out with both feet. They caught Wentworth behind the knees and he pitched backward, staggering, brought up hard against the wall. His saber was jarred out of his hand... but Colonel Rice stepped back, dropped his point. His face was flashed with anger.

"Confound you, Smithers!" he snapped at his adjutant. "Is that the kind of fair play they taught you at West Point!"

Wentworth had his saber again and flashed it in salute. "Sir," he said, "It is a pleasure to meet so honorable an opponent!"

Rice shook his head sharply. "I don't strike unarmed men!" he said flatly. "On guard!"

Once more the sabers clashed and now, gradually, Wentworth began to take the offensive. Colonel Rice was a little overconfident. On a parry, he left himself open to a shoulder cut, but Wentworth instead swung his saber from the wrist and his edge caught the colonel's blade just above the hilt. It was a powerful and smoothly executed blow, and Rice stepped back—his saber rang on the floor.

Wentworth smiled, caught up the sword and presented it hilt first. "On guard, Colonel Rice," he said. "Honors are evening up!"

Rice caught the saber, saluted, and Wentworth sprang into a dazzling attack. His sword was everywhere. A button leaped from the colonel's coat; the fabric was slashed on the shoulder, but so lightly that the flesh was not touched. Then once more the saber was driven from his hand.

Both men were panting, heavily. Perspiration made little crooked traces down from their temples. The force of his breathing made Wentworth's mouth corners tight, drew them back slightly from his teeth. Colonel Rice accepted his sword once more. There were no words this time, only the formal flash of the blades in salute, then once more the whir and dash of tempered steel.

A moment later, the sword of Colonel Rice flew high into the

Along the street marched a dragging file of men and
women, each bearing placards on their backs.

air, crashed against the wall and thudded to the floor. He was flat
against the wall with the point of Wentworth's saber to his chest.

"I don't wish to hurt you, Colonel Rice," Wentworth said
hoarsely. "You are outpointed, sir. Will you surrender?"

Rice's blue eyes were blazing and muscles knotted along his jaw. "I have never surrendered yet," he said thickly.

"We are not enemies," Wentworth urged. "We are on the same side, the side of honor and justice and the law! There was a bargain. We need such men as you!"

He dropped his sword point, tossed the weapon to the desk and held out his hand. For moments longer, the eyes of the two men held, then a smirk strained Colonel Rice's lips. He clasped Wentworth's hand warmly.

"You are the better man, Wentworth," he said simply. "It will be a pleasure to serve under you! I'll phone my resignation, confirm it by a letter left here. But I will not be a traitor to my commander!"

Wentworth bowed. "I ask no more, and you won't regret the decision. Be at…" He leaned close and whispered into the colonel's ear the place of rendezvous. "Either I or my men will meet you there."

He pivoted toward the door, unlocked it. A dozen men in khaki stood outside, bayonets fixed. They stared in amazement at Wentworth and beyond him to the colonel. Rice's voice reached out to them crisply.

"Release all prisoners into Major Wentworth's custody at once," he ordered. He closed the door then.

Amazement held Wentworth in his tracks for a moment. It was more than he had dared to hope, but he took instant advantage of the order.

"Sergeant," he said briskly. "Form your men. You will escort the prisoners to one of your armored trucks… You have one?

Good. At once, please. I will want four men as a guard to the city limits. I'll wait here,"

The sergeant saluted, though his eyes rested curiously on the saber cut on Wentworth's cheek, and briskly marched his men along the long corridor and to a flight of steel steps.

FIVE MINUTES dragged past while Wentworth waited casually outside the colonel's door. He lighted a cigarette, sucked the smoke deep into his lungs. Technically, of course, the colonel could not resign while on active duty. He would be called on to turn his command over to his junior, probably. Seconds were precious, but an attempt to hurry the freeing of the prisoners would increase the obvious suspicions of the men and probably excite immediate action. But Wentworth's ears were keenly attuned to sounds below and, presently, he caught the measured tread of marching men. His eyes strained down the hall, and he caught a deep breath of relief.

They were bringing the prisoners and, foremost among them, marched Nita van Sloan and Sailor Joe! Ten prisoners, some of them with cruddy bandaged wounds. Joe had a bloody cloth about his head but, though the eyes of the ten clung to him, none of them spoke. Wentworth's eyes met Nita's but he said nothing. Moments later, they were crowded, standing, into a truck. One soldier took the wheel, the others took their posts at the rear. Wentworth entered the cab and gave quiet directions to the driver.

A fraction of a second after the truck had swung around the first corner, motorcycles sirened their way to a halt before the armory. Wentworth saw the driver's eyes regarding him covertly, and the truck trundled too slowly along the street. Wentworth acted instantly. With a deft movement, he whipped the man's automatic from its holster.

"Stop the truck!" he ordered.

The man stared, mouth sagging, into the leveled muzzle of the gun and obeyed instantly. As the brakes took hold, Wentworth jabbed stiff, merciful fingers against nerve centers in the man's throat. He stumped, instantly unconscious, behind the wheel. It was the work of a moment to drag him from behind the wheel and start the truck on its way again.

Wentworth jammed the accelerator to the floor, twisted around the first corner, sped wildly through the dark streets. He was frowning with hard concentration. It looked very much as if Rice had been trapped before he could leave the armory. If that were so, he would have to send men to free the colonel.

He peered over his shoulder. There was a glass panel in the rear of the cab and, pressed against it, was the face of Sailor Joe! Wentworth motioned him back and, with a backhanded blow of the automatic, smashed out the glass.

"Overpower those men!" he snapped.

Sailor Joe winked a cheerful blue eye "Begging the skipper's pardon," he said with a grin, " 'tis already done!"

Wentworth laughed. It was good to have subordinates like Sailor Joe! But it was probably Nita who had ordered that it be done. A swift question revealed that four of the men besides Sailor Joe were in condition for active duty.

"When I check at the next corner, you five drop out," Wentworth ordered briskly. "Take the soldier's arms and uniforms, go

66

back and make sure that Colonel Rice gets away. He has enlisted for the duration of the war—with us! You know the rendezvous. Here's another prisoner in the cab."

When he checked the truck again, Nita ran forward and slid into the cab beside him. "All ready, Dick," she said quietly. "Sailor Joe is on his way."

Wentworth sent the truck surging forward again, and Nita's hand rested for an instant on his where it gripped the wheel. "I knew you'd get us free, Dick, if you were… if you were spared. We were ready to march out of the cavern camp, when the Black Police struck. We didn't have much chance. It was…. horrible."

Wentworth flung a quick smile toward her. "They're already been paid in full for that—at Titustown," he said quietly, "if there's any satisfaction in that. The Master keeps us so busy defending ourselves, we have small opportunity to plan to find and remove him. It's good strategy."

His words were light, but his voice was grave and there was a heavy weight about his heart. His status, and that of the outlawed men he captained, was becoming increasingly precarious. If they had found the cavern, well hidden as it was, they might easily discover the Catskill and Peekskill encampments. After that, the end would not be far away. This was not a battle which could be fought by one man alone as so often the Spider had done before. It called for detailed organization, strong forces of quick-moving men.

Nita spoke hesitantly. "The other camps—they are safe?"

"At last reports, an hour ago," Wentworth told her, "but the messenger I started for Washington was caught and hanged.

We've dispatched another, but God knows whether he'll get through."

Nita said quickly, "Washington is investigating, I know that! A man disguised as one of the Black Police came to our cell an hour ago. He had a G-man's credentials, and his name was Miller. He wanted to get a message through to you."

"What did you tell him!"

Nita shook her head. "Nothing at all, of course. The papers were all right—his credentials I mean—but we were afraid to take a chance."

"G-man Miller," Wentworth mused. "I hope to God Washington is taking up our battle! I'm afraid that escaping from the state to carry information there will be almost impossible. The entire state is doubly guarded, under quarantine because of the plague...."

The words died on his lips. Along the street ahead of him marched a dragging file of men and women. Each of them carried a tiny bell which he rang incessantly and on their backs were placards which read:

PLAGUE
WE FOUGHT THE BLACK POLICE.

Their guard of Black Police marched a half block behind and ahead of them, armed with rifles, although flight was impossible for the prisoners. They were chained together. Wentworth's foot hovered over the brake... But what could he do against the plague? Those poor victims would soon be beyond fear or danger from the criminals! His anger hardened in his breast. It was cowardly to flee to the safety of the hills while the Black Police rode roughshod over the people!

By a rigid effort, he controlled himself. He did not have sufficient men necessary to sweep the Black Police and the Master from power. Failing in that, it would be suicidal to attempt a minor foray. But there would be retribution! Tonight was not the time. The entire city would be in arms within a short while—probably already the Black Police were organizing a search for their vanished prisoners. They must flee now, but tomorrow, another night, he would return....

WENTWORTH BRAKED the truck, whipped up a side street and from that into the entrance of a warehouse. The door thundered shut behind him, and Wentworth threw open the door. The bent figure of the old soldier, Brace, hurried toward him.

"Congratulations, commander," he said quietly, "but we knew you'd do it. Sailor Joe phoned they were successful and were on their way here with Colonel Rice. Perrin already has left with anti-toxin for the cavern. And we have a few prisoners for you. Two captains of the Black Police, whose records we can give you, and the judge who condemned two senators to death on false evidence!"

"Excellent," Wentworth replied. "Keep up the raids. I'll send you ten more men who are not known to the police. Destroy this truck. We'll make the rest of the trip in passenger cars, with the prisoners. I'll give you an order on Jackson, commander at Catskill—for the men. We're going to Peekskill." He started to turn toward Nita, but something grave in Brace's face stopped him. He faced the old soldier. "Something else to report, Brace?" he asked quietly.

Brace nodded heavily. "It's news I hate to give, sir. There was a phone call a few minutes ago. Peekskill has been raided by the Black Police. Our people succeeded in fighting the raid off, but the losses were terrible. They abandoned the camp, took to the hills. And… there's plague among them."

Wentworth ripped out a harsh oath. "Anti-toxin…" he began.

Brace nodded. "We divided the supply, sir, and I took the liberty of sending a batch down there, but there's not nearly enough though we cleaned out the hospital. And, sir, there's more ill news."

Wentworth swung heavily down from the truck and felt Nita's hand come to rest on his arm. They had faced many defeats together, but this was worse than all the others. Two of his camps destroyed. God alone knew if the third was threatened. If that went, too… He braced his shoulders with an effort. If only they could get word through to Washington and win Federal intervention. But he was not too hopeful of that. As yet, the state authorities had been careful to provide no opening for Federal action—had covered their violence well.

"The rest of your news, Brace?" he said harshly.

"The second messenger to Washington was caught, too, sir. Secret agents overtook him in Delaware and… and killed him." The man's gray head came up suddenly. "I was sure he'd get through for you, sir. I drilled him well."

"You, Brace?"

Brace said, dully, "He was my son, sir."

Nita uttered a little cry of sympathy and moved to Brace's side. "Oh, I'm so terribly sorry. Those scoundrels in the Capitol! Oh, Dick—we're beaten! There's nothing left except to break through the state borders and flee this terrible place before we're all killed or stricken with the plague."

Her eyes pleaded with him, but the steely glint in Brace's gaze was inflexible. Wentworth put his hand on the man's shoulder. "Vengeance is a feeble thing to replace a son," be said, "but you shall have that, at least. And you shall have your reward when this state is made clean again. But I can't ask any more men to make that try at Washington." He drew in a slow breath. "Send word to Kirkpatrick at the cavern," he went on, his voice crisping. "Sailor Joe will relieve him there and Kirkpatrick will join Jackson at Catskill, and take command in my place. Brace, you shall have fifty men for raids—instead of ten. Nita, Catskill for you, too. Hold all prisoners there until I return to try them for their crimes."

"Return?" Nita cried. "Oh, Dick...."

Wentworth's lips drew thinly together. "I'm going to Washington," he said quietly.

WENTWORTH MET opposition from his own men in his determination. Sailor Joe volunteered to make the effort, but in the end Wentworth had his way. It already had been proved that ordinary methods would not serve to escape from the state. Even if that were achieved, there was still the peril of the secret agents of the Master, now apparently spread over the entire East. It was not the first time that men outside of New York had been found by the vengeful agents of the Black Police. If

FATHER FLOWER

SAILOR JOE

KIRKPATRICK

Washington could be persuaded to act, it would mean a sudden cessation of the tyranny. Wentworth knew that to achieve the same thing independently might require months, if indeed it could be accomplished at all.

It was midnight when, all arrangements made, Wentworth

G·MAN MILLER

GOVERNOR WHITING

COLONEL RICE

left the rendezvous and drove alone toward the Albany airport. Ships there undoubtedly would be under strong guard, but it was his best bet. Ordinarily, he would have chosen to try one of the smaller fields scattered over the state, but the Black Police long since had concentrated ships at a few central points. The

Master had early recognized the danger they might constitute in the wrong hands.

Wentworth made a wide circuit of the airport district and approached the field itself through a woods, on foot. There was small chance that he could force the hangars single-handed, but he had other plans. He had chosen the down-wind end of the field. Any ships that took off would have to taxi to a point near him before making their up-wind run. There would be a few moments, while the plane was maneuvering a turn, when the pilot's attention was entirely centered on his craft—and when it would be comparatively easy to overcome him. So Wentworth hoped....

For two hours, Wentworth waited in his covert for the chance. Several planes landed, and one took off, but at a point too remote to make an attack feasible. Wentworth had almost determined to attempt a raid on the hangar when a small-winged, swift craft was rolled out and the engine started on its warm-up.

Outlined against the hangar lights, Wentworth could see the pilot, clad in the uniform of the Black Police, as he shouldered parachute straps and pulled on a helmet. Grimly, Wentworth gathered himself in the shadows. His hand moved tentatively to an automatic, but he waited.

After a long dragging while, the pilot climbed into the cockpit of the plane and sent it trundling down the field. If this chance also failed... but it must not! Wentworth rose to his feet. The plane obviously was not coming as close as he had hoped. No matter—it must serve. The ship was almost opposite him now and better than a hundred yards away. In a moment the pilot would, throw the tail around and take off.

Wentworth sprang from his cover, like a sprinter from the mark, and raced toward the ship. It would take him eleven, perhaps twelve seconds to reach the plane....

Wentworth's eyes held steadily on the pilot. If the man should spot him.... The plane was handled expertly and a quick roar of the motors, a kick at the rudder threw it nose-on to the wind. Wentworth was still fifty yards from the ship when the field floodlights blazed on. He was fully revealed in that instant and saw the pilot's head whip toward him. In the next moment, gun flame lanced toward Wentworth! The ship began to trundle slowly forward!

Wentworth whipped his automatic from its holster and, in the same instant, checked his forward race. He squeezed off a single shot, then was sprinting forward again. The plane still rolled on, but no more gun-flame spewed toward him. The pilot's head had disappeared below the edge. Was it trickery, or had the bullet sped true? Deliberately, as he darted after the slowly moving ship, Wentworth threw another bullet through the fabric of the fuselage at the cockpit.

The pilot lunged into sight. His cry echoed hoarsely, a strange lorn sound across the beat of the engine. Other guns were spitting now from the hangars. A motorcycle was racing toward Wentworth. He threw all his strength into a final effort and reached the wing of the plane. When he threw his weight upon it, the ship slewed in its course, wavered for a moment and almost ground-looped. Then Wentworth was beside the cockpit. He seized the pilot by the shoulders, heaved and tossed him to the ground. He flung himself into the pilot's seat, wrenched the throttle wide.

Guns were still smashing out near the hangar. The motor-cycle was racing to intercept him and he caught the glitter of a mounted machine gun on its side-cart! Wentworth leaned wide over the side and pumped out three bullets from his automatic. He thought be heard lead *pinnng* on his propeller, but couldn't be sure. He saw the operator of the motorcycle bullet-hammered from his saddle. The machine slewed wildly and, just short of it, Wentworth wrenched the plane into the air. Moments later, he began a swift climbing spiral toward the black sky.

Twice, he circled the field. Already, they were running out a ship to pursue him, but he knew it would be minutes before the motor could be warmed. By that time… A chill of alarm touched Wentworth. Surely, there was something wrong with his engine!

He listened more acutely and spotted the trouble. He had not been wrong about a bullet striking the propeller. Its vibration was uneven. Already, he could feel the tremor of the ship. Impossible to estimate how long it would last, but he knew the vibration would increase rapidly as the wind of its rotation tore at the warped and punctured propeller. The end would come suddenly. A wrench as the propeller tore loose, a wild engine ripping loose from its mountings—*and he wore no parachute!*

CHAPTER 5
THE LONG BLACK ARM

WITH THE certainty of disaster heavy upon him, Wentworth studied the night-black skies and tried to make plans. Already the pursuing plane was preparing to take off from the Albany field. A battle with the pilot and headlong flight were equally out of the question. By throttling the motor down, Wentworth still had a chance to keep the ship in the air until the state border was passed. But that meant disaster, as surely as did the damaged propeller. He would be overtaken, shot down....

As the only alternative, Wentworth held the plane at a steep climb. He would soar as high as the steadily increasing vibration would permit. When it became too great, he would have to cut his motor and glide with a dead stick toward the border—hope against hope that he would succeed in passing the guards. If the pursuit managed to keep him in sight and climbed more rapidly... Wentworth lifted his shoulders in a slight shrug. It was not fatalism, but grim readiness to meet whatever blows destiny might deal to hurt, when they befell, and to the best of his ability.

Gripping the stick between his knees, Wentworth made sure his automatics were fully loaded and ready. Afterward he divided his attention between the laboring motor and the pursuit. The floodlights below blacked out—the other ship was in the air! At the same moment, Wentworth realized that he must cut the speed of the engine, or rip his plane to bits. Reluctantly, he eased the throttle. It was the first step toward failure. He would

77

be compelled to repeat that action with mounting frequency until finally the engine would sustain the plane no more. Then... flight's end.

Abruptly, Wentworth formed a resolution. Without lights in this black sky, he could be spotted only by the flame of his exhaust. He dared not kill his motor, but he throttled it so low it barely turned over. His altimeter showed three thousand feet. He could glide for a mile, perhaps five, according to the wind. By that time, pursuit should have swept past. Then he could open the throttle, climb again—and repeat the process as long as the racked motor held together.

It was a desperate chance Wentworth took, with the absolute certainty of death if he were spotted by the high-flying machine-gun-armed police plane behind him. The only thing in his favor was that the other pilot would expect headlong flight... Minutes dragged past while the plane slid through the air, the prop barely turning, the whine of wind among the struts clearly audible above the muffled engine. Presently, Wentworth's straining ears caught the sound for which he waited—the bellowing roar of a plane driven at full speed. It flashed past two thousand feet overhead, its exhaust a scarlet gash, a blazing comet's tail against the sky.

Wentworth held the glide as long as he dared, until the up-reaching tops of trees seemed to brush the fuselage, then cracked the throttle again. The motor faltered a little before it picked up, and a crack-up was perilously close before Wentworth dared once more to pull up the ship's nose. He put the plane into a slow climb, the motor very little above stalling speed. The least fluke of the wind might throw him into a spin from which he could not escape because the ground was so close. But even at this reduced pace, the engine labored and the vibration of the distorted prop threatened dissolution.

Seeming hours dragged past while Wentworth fought the loggy plane slowly higher. There would be air patrols, searchlights at the state's border. Even as the thought crossed Wentworth's mind, he saw the focused blue-white beams lick out at the sky. They were like monster legs, crossing, kicking apart in a soundless, stately tap-dance—or like groping fingers combing the blackness of the sky. Now and again they prodded an insect-plane of the patrol into sight, clung to it an instant for identification, then flicked carelessly on.

Altitude was Wentworth's only chance, and he could not hope to climb high enough to evade those lights. Once he was spotted, the killer planes would converge upon him. Wentworth's glance flicked to his altimeter which registered five thousand feet. The chart showed the Delaware River a bare mile beyond the border here.

Swiftly, Wentworth made his decision. Instantly, he put the nose of the plane down and cut the motor, killed it. He dived steeply. A mile to the border and, a mile beyond that, was the Delaware River. No motor sound at all now—only the whistle of the wind-revolved propeller, the whining struts. There was a bare possibility that, nearly silent, he might glide across the border undetected—except if a light struck him. His dive should give him a speed of nearly two hundred miles an hour, even with the motor dead. It wouldn't take long, after he crossed the border, to reach the river. But if he were spotted, during that brief hop to the river, he would be a dead, helpless target for the machine-guns!

Nearer and nearer swept the lights. As if they knew of his approach, they seemed to sweep in more furious pirouettes across the sky—already in a dance of savage triumph. Wentworth's lips drew thin and cold against his teeth. He hunched forward, then smiled mirthlessly and forced himself to relax. He touched his automatic briefly... A hundred yards away, a thousand feet below, the eye of a searchlight abruptly winked directly into his dazzled gaze!

WENTWORTH HELD his plane steadily on its way. He had no choice with that dead motor. The light pinned him for a long second, then another flashed across the sky, and another. He was embraced in a thousand broken nettles of light, thrusting up past the wings, finding tiny apertures in the floor of the fuselage. It seemed to Wentworth that they were tangibly gripping, holding the plane. He heard the heavy, slow stammer of high-caliber machine guns on the earth and, like a bird of prey's scream, the high whine of a diving plane behind him.

Frantically, Wentworth thrust down the nose of his ship and broke the glide in which he had swept across the border. His only escape from those lights lay close to the earth where they could not follow. He kicked the rudder and, numbly, heard the drumbeat of machine-gun bullets on the taut fabric of the left wing. Then, abruptly, he was in darkness. The swords of the lights crossed over his head. His eyes were blinded, and he peered desperately toward the earth. How far below was it now? For long seconds, he could see nothing. Then, incredibly close, the tossing green top of a tree made itself visible below him. It was stirring with the wind of his passage!

Desperately, Wentworth used some of the force of his dive in a powerless zoom, banked off to the right and straightened out once more on the course for the river. A parachute flare blossomed into chemical brilliance overhead. The shadows of the trees were black shifting canyons among high-lighted green. Ahead, a deeper, blacker canyon loomed—the river! But the planes were diving again, machine guns perforating the high shout of the wind. Wentworth's speed was wasted, the ship moving ahead slowly. In swift despair, Wentworth thrust forward the stick and swept down toward the trees!

It was not the completely mad, blind maneuver it seemed. Through the trees, he had caught the glint of water where a creek tumbled down a ravine toward the near-by river. If he could strike through that, even though wings were snapped off, the ship should catapult through to the deeper water of the river itself. He hoped… Machine-gun bullets plucked across the fuselage behind him. The instrument board shivered to bits. The whole plane shuddered under the assault of the lead. In frantic pantomime, Wentworth surged upward in the cockpit, then drooped forward limply as if the flying lead had pierced him through.

An instant later, the plane swept into the black canyon of the ravine. Limbs tagged the undercarriage, the wings threshed against saplings. With precise, deliberate fingers, Wentworth unbuckled his safety belt. In the dying light of the flare, he could see the black, ominous breast of the river a hundred feet ahead. The right wing struck a tree, and the plane started to loop. Another tree caught the left wing. The weighted fuselage lunged on, glanced off the soft earth of the embankment and made a frantic leap, turned it into a dive as the motor dragged it down.

Wentworth saw the river reach up for the plane. Dazedly, he tensed his legs beneath him and, in the instant before the motor clove the water, he flung himself out into space. Wentworth tried to steady himself in the brief moment of his passage through the air—strove to strike feet-first. He was only partly successful. The surface reached up and struck him like a sledge-hammer. It drove the wind from him, hammered his senses into numbness. Paralyzed, he sluiced down through water into icy coldness sword-sharp.

Somehow he got his hands above his head, planed along below the surface. His feet scraped jarringly along the bottom, his legs bent and his whole body slammed down with the force of a rough parachute landing but it was no more than that. Dazedly, Wentworth knew that he had escaped serious injury. But his muscles still refused to obey the summons of his will.

The swift current already had caught him up and the natural buoyancy of his body was floating him upward. Feebly, he achieved a kick—a faltering stroke with his arms. After an eternity, his head burst out into the air.

He drew a sobbing breath and let the water carry him. He could do little more. The paralysis of the cold seized him when shock began to recede....

He drifted.

THE SPIDER AT BAY

THERE WAS a period when things went completely dark in his brain. When, finally, memory began to function again, he was half out of the jostling river and clinging to an exposed root of a tree. Feebly, he dragged himself ashore.

He drove himself to his feet, with the help of a fragment of a dead tree branch, and, with that for support, fought his way through thick woods. Gradually, as he struggled on, his limbs began to move more freely. It was close to dawn when he spotted a ramshackle hay-barn and managed to push out of sight in its welcome warmth. Then exhaustion claimed him.

It was dark again when Wentworth dragged himself out of the barn. He was sore, weak from hunger and exposure, but he had made good his escape... it seemed. Wentworth stumbled presently upon a farmhouse and managed to persuade the family to feed him. More than that he dared not risk, lest they suspect that he was other than his unshaven cheeks and ruined clothing indicated—a tramp.

It was hours later that he reached a railroad, and other hours before he reached a siding where he could steal aboard a freight train. He continued the role he had assumed, for it seemed to Wentworth less dangerous than an attempt to purchase new clothing and rehabilitate his appearance.

Without doubt, the Master had many spies in Washington, and they would be alert and watching for him. The Master would not permit his apparent death to be taken for granted!

WITH THAT in mind, Wentworth in the two days that followed, made steady progress to the west and south until he had circled Washington and could enter from the south. Only then did he dare to enter a barber shop and purchase new clothing.

He delayed overnight to buy a secondhand car and license plates in a town in the Valley of Virginia, and then struck out again for Washington. But his task was only half completed when he actually had entered the city. The strongest guards would be thrown about the very offices to which he must penetrate, if he were to gain official help against the Master and the Black Police. For that, only one thing would serve: Wentworth must somehow get through to the President himself!

In his own identity, that would not be too difficult. He had rendered signal services to the government in some of his many battles against the underworld, but... Wentworth dared not announce himself! The instant he did, the Master's entire spy system would be at work to track him down and prevent the interview! The capture and execution of Brace's son, beyond the boundaries of New York State, showed the efficacy of their organization.

As he drove steadily through the streets of Washington, Wentworth could not escape a feeling of bitterness. On these thoroughfares, people walked and rode in freedom. Men stood laughing in corner groups. Their shoulders and heads were carried erectly.

Until he saw them, Wentworth had not realized completely the pall the Master had laid upon New York. There men moved always with a certain furtiveness or, if they were allies of the Black Police, walked with a conscious and oppressive swagger. What smiles came to men's lips were arrogant or fawning, and of healthy laughter, there was none at all. And on top of that had come this foul and man-created plague....

The goading demand for instant and radical action against the powers that could so oppress the people Wentworth loved rode him cruelly and it was with difficulty that he forced himself once more to patience. He registered at a small hotel under a false name and bought a newspaper before he went to his room to make his plans. He had hoped to learn from the paper no more than the President's plans for the day but abruptly he was startled by the black headlines. They concerned a trial in New York State....

FOUR POLICE CONFESS SPIDER BRIBED THEM
OFFICERS BROUGHT TO TRIAL BY GOVER-
NOR—PUT BLAME FOR OUTRAGES IN STATE
UPON OUTLAWED CRIMINAL

For a long moment, Wentworth could not tear his eyes from those headlines, then he skimmed through the story and a slow rage ate its hot way through his veins.

Several high officials of the Black Police had been brought to trial in a "purge" that was a replica of the wholesale executions of the Soviets. Well Wentworth knew the machinery of such travesties of justice. Through threats to their families, through torture, men were compelled to say on the witness stand whatever the government wished. In this case, the intention was clear enough. The Master was going to lay the blame for the lawless plundering of the state squarely on Wentworth's shoulders! He ran through the list of the crimes confessed by the men "in betrayal of the public trust and of the oath sworn before the governor." One and all were blamed directly upon the orders of the Spider!

With hands that shook a little, in spite of his iron control, Wentworth slowly folded the paper and placed it carefully upon the desk. He had to make himself do these routine things slowly lest his anger burst beyond his control!

He needed no explanation of the reasons that had actuated the Master. This was a deliberate attempt to discredit in advance anything Wentworth might manage to communicate to Washington! Wentworth had spoken truly when he had said that the Master struck so rapidly and shrewdly that the outlaws had time for little except defense! According to the newspaper, Governor Whiting had issued a personal appeal to the people to destroy their malefactor, the Spider, and the cooperation of all neighboring states was requested in apprehending him....

ABRUPTLY, WENTWORTH whipped toward the door. There was no reason for footsteps in this hallway to be so soft and furtive. He had heard the muted tread of several men. His constantly attuned senses told him that they stood motionless, listening now, just outside his door. A small and pursed smile touched his lips. Briefly, his hands touched the automatics beneath his arms. They had tracked him very quickly, these spies of the Master!

He shook his head sharply. He was leaping too rapidly to conclusions! What was much more likely was that the secret police of the Master had traced him—and then demanded *federal* help in his arrest!

All this flashed through Wentworth's mind in the pregnant moment between the cessation of sounds in the hallway and the first, commanding knuckle-rap upon the door. It caused him to whip his hand from his gun and spring to the window. He saw instantly that there was no escape that way. He darted into the bathroom and swiftly crouched before the inter-connecting door which led to the next room. A steel implement in his fingers moved swiftly, and the lock gave. Behind him, a man knocked more loudly.

Wentworth shouted from the doorway, "Wait a minute!"

He opened the faucets in the tub and, while water poured noisily into it, he slid through into the next room. It was fortunately empty. He reached the hall door in two strides and opened it, stepped outside. There were four Washington city police and a plainclothesman outside the door of his own room. Wentworth stared at them with well-feigned curiosity.

"Who you pinching?" he asked in a hoarse whisper.

One of the cops swung toward him, "Beat it!" he ordered, whispering, too. "There may be lead flying here in a minute!"

"Yeah? Who you pinching?" Wentworth repeated.

The cop took a threatening step toward him, and Wentworth scuttled along the hallway, but kept staring back until he reached the steps. He went down them rapidly. It wouldn't take them many seconds after their entrance to figure his mode of escape… If he had needed any substantiation of the danger he underwent, it had been provided!

Wentworth hurried to a sight-seeing tour center and bought a ticket for a two-hour trip around the city. Then he settled himself on the bus to make plans… As a result, when the sight-seeing tour finally entered the White House grounds, Wentworth managed to separate himself and remain concealed among the shrubbery. It was the last trip of the day, but even so Wentworth had an hour's wait for darkness.

The grounds were patrolled and the house closely guarded, but Wentworth had broken into more difficult places than this. Dinner was being prepared in the kitchen and many people moved back and forth, so the door was not locked. Wentworth merely walked openly and purposefully through the service hall. He nodded absently when one of the servants glanced toward him, feigned preoccupation as he moved on. If Wentworth had hesitated or appeared in the least uncertain, he would have been challenged. As it was, the servant went back to his work, and Wentworth was within the sacred precincts of the White House.

He knew his way thoroughly—as he always did when once he had been a guest in a house—and made his way without hesitation to the office in which the President was wont to work after dinner. He was waiting there when the President entered….

"I'm Richard Wentworth, Mr. President," he said quietly, and rose with a deliberate bow.

THE PRESIDENT'S intelligent eyes swept Wentworth's face with a quick, comprehensive scrutiny. A lesser man might have challenged even a personal acquaintance who had forced his way into this sanctum, unannounced, but the President, after that single look, moved deliberately to his chair behind the desk.

"It's slightly irregular," he said with his quick, pleasant smile, "but you undoubtedly have your reasons, Mr. Wentworth. I have had occasion to be grateful to you on one or two occasions."

Wentworth had not been aware until that moment that he was holding his breath. He let it out softly. "Thank you, sir," he said, quietly, "I won't waste time. I don't know how much time I have. How familiar are you with affairs in New York State?"

The President, now seated, was openly studying him. "I'm not sure," he said. "I have had reports, but they are contradictory. I was contemplating a request that Governor Whiting visit me here, when these trials started. They are strangely reminiscent of Moscow. On the other hand, Mr. Wentworth, my reports say that you have openly used the seal of the Spider. To the Spider, on occasion, the government has owed much. Frankly, you have placed me in a very difficult position by coming here."

"That is one reason I came as I did, sir," Wentworth said swiftly. "The other reason, that I did not simply request an interview...."

"Yes?" the President prompted, as Wentworth hesitated.

"I'll be frank, too, sir," Wentworth said steadily. "I was not sure whether the criminals who control New York State would not intercept that message—and reach me first!"

A slight weariness touched the President's face. "Yes, you may be right," he conceded. "I've lost many people I used to lean upon. Tell me now about your state."

He leaned back in his chair, closed his eyes, while Wentworth crisply recounted the oppressions inflicted upon the people—torture, murder, extortion. He told how the few people, who dared to oppose the Black Police, had banded together under his leadership—and he also told of the coming of the plague.

"Two men I dispatched to you, sir, with messages," Wentworth concluded, "were killed out of hand. It became necessary for me to come in person. I've been three nights and three days getting here...."

The President opened his eyes. His face was stern and deep lines curved downward about his mouth. "It is infamous!" he cried ringingly. "Short of armed intervention, it would seem almost impossible to overthrow such a combine! If I were to order a regiment there...."

"You would be impeached overnight," Wentworth supplied softly. "I know, sir! If any rumors of affairs there have been leaking out, as they must have, these trials and 'confessions' will put the sole blame on my shoulders. As long as federal prerogatives are not interfered with, you cannot act. And they are very careful about those. But if you could send federal agents there to investigate, to make a report to Congress?"

"Congress!" The President smiled faintly. "Yes, something might be accomplished that way. This is what I am going to do, Mr. Wentworth. I will try to compel a new election in New York State and I'll order some navy ships to the Hudson for 'maneuvers.' It would be possible to warn Governor Whiting that, unless lawlessness is stamped out, we will be compelled to take some action to protect our leading port."

Wentworth sprang to his feet, "It's more than I had dared to hope for, Mr. President!"

The President said dryly, "It may be more than I can accomplish. I'll try! Now...."

Abruptly, the door of the President's office was thrown wide, and three armed White House guards jammed into the entrance. Their guns covered Wentworth.

"Your pardon, Mr. President," the leader said. "One of the cooks reported seeing a fellow come in. Put up your hands, man. We'll shoot, if you stir!"

Wentworth lifted his hands slowly. Under his breath, he whispered to the President, "Denounce me, sir! Say I held a gun on you! You can't permit your political enemies to say you allowed me here—a criminal and murderer!"

The leading guard was moving warily toward Wentworth, gun ready, and Wentworth was forced to cut his whisper short.

"You came just in time," he said harshly. "You slaves of tyranny! Another thirty seconds, and I would have fixed this bloody-sucking capitalist so he couldn't oppress the people any longer!"

CHAPTER 6
VOTE DOWN THE PLAGUE!

I T WAS incredible, under the circumstances, to hear the President break into a deep and hearty laugh! The heads of the guards swung toward him in amazement and, for an instant, Wentworth hovered on the brink of leaping upon them. But it might endanger the President's life, and God knew the nation needed him as never before in these days!

"I appreciate your zealous work, Marlowe," the President said pleasantly to the leader of the guards, "and it's true that Mr. Wentworth was somewhat informal in his manner of calling. No, no, put away your guns. Mr. Wentworth will have his little joke."

He turned to Wentworth, and his face was grave. "I appreciate your intention, but, if my willingness to hear complaints against tyranny are ammunition against me then let my enemies use it! To the best of my ability, Mr. Wentworth, I'll fulfill my promise!" He held out his hand.

Wentworth felt a deep reverence for the President's courage, though, under the circumstances, he considered it foolhardy. He grasped the hand warmly.

"Thank you, sir," he said. "I'm going back now."

"It's a task I don't envy you," the President said, "but I admire your respect for your duty—the more since it is self-imposed. Marlowe, place a car and a guard at Mr. Wentworth's disposal. Good night, sir, and thank you."

Wentworth carried his elation with him for a full five minutes. Then he discovered that the sedan in which he left the White House was trailed by another car. His lips settled into a grim mold then, but his hope refused to be crushed. Even with the unfair tactics which the Master would employ, any election called in New York State should sweep Governor Whiting and the Black Police out of power. There was some question of whether the President would be able to enforce his will—considerable question. But the mere threat of federal interference should do a great deal to alleviate conditions for the people of New York....

Wentworth's head whipped about and his hand half-lifted to his automatic as the trailing limousine sped past. There were five men in the car, and their glares concentrated on him. Wentworth laughed softly and lifted his hat to them. He had no immediate fears. Even the minions of the Master would scarcely dare to attack a Presidential car. It would be unwise....

At the airport to which Wentworth directed the car, he made immediate arrangements to charter a plane for Albany. There was some demur, because of the plague, but finally the deal was completed... and the trailing crew of gunmen did not interfere. Their reason was plain enough. Things could be handled so much more satisfactorily in Albany, from their point of view!

Within five minutes of the take-off, Wentworth was aware of another ship, powerfully motored, which kept pace with them across the night sky. Five miles across the border of New York State, Wentworth lost them by the simple process of leaping over the side, and plunging without opening his parachute until dangerously close to the ground.

It was a repetition of his flight across country to Washington—except for two things. Here the Black Police patrolled constantly and therefore were on the lookout for him. But the people also knew the Spider for their friend and were eager to help him. A farmer got out his milk truck and drove Wentworth forty miles to a city where his men had a spy headquarters. When Wentworth entered the tiny magazine shop, the operator fell on his knees and tears trickled unashamed down his cheeks.

"The commander!" the man stammered. "The commander! They told us you were dead. Oh, thank God!"

WENTWORTH COMMANDEERED a motorcycle and drove it to within ten miles of the Catskill camp, where he abandoned the machine for a horse and pushed on through the back-lanes of the hills. He did not know how thoroughly the Black Police patrolled the district, but he would run no risk of capture. The news he bore was too heart-filling. Why, if the President achieved his promise, they were within a few weeks of freedom again! One thing could make victory sure—if they discovered the identity of the Master and destroyed him! No one else, Wentworth was sure, had the intelligence to defeat them at the polls....

With his thoughts to spur him, Wentworth pushed the horse at a steady pace into the hills. He paused presently in a night-black ravine and drew out a whistle on which he blew three shrill blasts. The embankments picked up the sound and sent it echoing ahead, and, moments later, a searchlight blazed down the cut. Then a man's almost inarticulate shout of joy sounded.

"The commander! It's the commander!"

His voice echoed and other voices picked it up, sent the news winging ahead as sentry after sentry relayed the news back to camp. A small grave smile tugged at Wentworth's lips. It was humbling to be so hailed. He had achieved so little in his cease-less warfare. It seemed to him that only failure lay behind, but with such loyal men... Wentworth spurred up the glade and past sentries whose faces creased in smiles of welcome. Their voices bore him along....

"Thank God you're back, commander!"

"They spread the word you were dead, commander!"

"We knew they couldn't kill you, commander!"

No lights could be shown within the fortress itself, but in the darkness men ran and called eagerly beside him. He was lifted from his horse and borne on their shoulders until he came to the porch of the log cabin headquarters. Two men met him there, and Wentworth clasped hands with Kirkpatrick and with Colonel Rice. Jackson stepped forward from the darkness to salute.

Wentworth turned to the white glimmer of up-turned faces before the porch and called to them softly. "I have seen the President," he said quietly. "He has promised to help in every way he can. Tomorrow, I will have plans for you."

He turned to Kirkpatrick. "The time has come to make our biggest play," he said. "We must kidnap Governor Whiting and force him to tell the identity of the Master!"

Kirkpatrick's lips curved in a faint smile, "We're one up on you, Dick," he said quietly. "We have the governor a prisoner here. But he either doesn't know who the Master is or else is too terrified to tell."

Wentworth's laugh was startled from him. "It's a good omen!" he cried. "Now I believe in victory again."

While he spoke, his eyes were questing in the darkness. It was inconceivable that Nita van Sloan should not meet him if she were here, and he knew a sharp moment of fear. Nothing had happened to her. It couldn't now, when so much that was good offered. Kirkpatrick understood that glance and the suppressed anxiety behind it.

"Our headquarters in New York was destroyed," he said quietly. "Nita went to set up a new place. We couldn't stop her. Sailor Joe and Ram Singh went with her."

Wentworth nodded wordlessly, though his heart leaped with anxiety for Nita. She should be well protected by those two men. "I think," he said softly, "that an interview with Governor Whiting is indicated."

He led the way then into the log cabin and, within blanketed windows, lights were turned on again. A man in a priest's black robe rose from beside the open fire and came toward him—a small man with a gentle face.

"We have missed you," he said simply.

"And I have missed you," Wentworth told him. He sucked in a chest-filling breath. "It's good to be back if only for a few hours."

Father Flower shook his head. "We have done evil things since you have been gone," he said. "Evil things though they were necessary. We have hanged fourteen men."

"Not our men!" Wentworth cried.

Colonel Rice's bluff, curt voice cut in. "Black Police. Prisoners. They were duly tried. Kirkpatrick defended them. Convicted, hanged… with the Spider's web. And delivered back to the towns in which they sinned. Every man we hanged was a murderer a half-dozen times over."

Wentworth frowned. He could not say it was ill done. It was such a course as he himself might have followed, though he had never yet killed a man who did not have opportunity to defend himself. It was completely just. But it was unfortunate at this time. It might make intercession by the President difficult.

"A forceful answer to their crimes," he said slowly, "but I think we should discontinue such punishments now if we are to get federal help." Briefly then he told of his interview with the President. "We must concentrate our attention on finding the Master. He can cancel out all our work unless we are rid of him before the election. I'd like to see the governor now."

JACKSON NODDED and, heaving up a trapdoor in the floor, called an order. Presently Governor Whiting was thrust up the steps by two armed men, each handcuffed to one of Whiting's wrists. The governor was a man of leonine mold and inclined to bluster but the strength was gone out of him now. His lips trembled and his eyes only touched Wentworth's in passing before they sank again to the floor.

"I protest against this outrage," he said weakly. "The state of New York will not tolerate this. I am the governor, sir!"

Wentworth allowed a slight, cold smile to move his lips. "You *were* the governor," he said. "Now you are a prisoner before a just court. Can you advance any reason why we shouldn't hang you as we have fourteen of your underlings? If they were guilty, you are separately guilty for each of them. They were appointed by you. They took your orders!"

Governor Whiting sagged to his knees. "As God is my witness," he whispered, "I have never ordered a human being harmed or killed! Please, you won't harm me? I've only taken orders myself, from a man I don't know—but who threatened to kill me, horribly, if I didn't obey. You can't kill me for that. Not just because I was afraid! For God's sake, say you won't kill me! Anything but that! I'll be your slave—"

"Shut him up!" Wentworth said curtly.

He felt sickened. This cowardly groveling creature had been elected governor of the state and had surrendered it to criminals. Death? Yes, certainly he deserved death a hundred times over. He had wrought the deaths of many better men. There was no need now for the guards to shut him up. Whiting closed his trembling lips, but his eyes begged for him.

"One thing can save you," Wentworth said coldly. "If you speak again, tell us the name of the man you serve—the Master! Otherwise…."

Jackson caught Wentworth's brief gesture and dropped a noose about Whiting's neck. He started like a bee-stung horse and an inarticulate cry rose in his throat.

"No, no!" he gasped. "If I knew I would tell! I swear I would. I only see a… a white face in a mirror!"

There was disgust on the faces of Kirkpatrick and Colonel Rice, and Wentworth knew that his own mirrored their expression. He said heavily, "I suppose he's telling the truth."

Kirkpatrick and Rice nodded deliberately. The colonel said crisply, "He's no more good to us, or to the state. I vote for death! Such a coward doesn't deserve to live!"

Abruptly, the door of the cabin flung open and a sentry burst in, stiffened to salute. "Commander! Party of our men coming with a blindfolded prisoner. Says he's G-man Miller and has a message for you!"

Wentworth's eyes narrowed at the news. He remembered

that Nita, when he had freed her from the Black Police, had mentioned a federal agent of that name. It was possible, of course, that he brought word from Washington.

"In five minutes," he agreed shortly, and turned back to Governor Whiting. "Trial adjourned. We will discuss your fate later. I would advise you, Whiting, to improve your memory a little. If you could think of any little thing that would help us to find the Master, we may be more inclined to leniency. Take him below."

He turned his back on the wretched man's babblings and moved to a table where he dropped into a chair. Kirkpatrick and Colonel Rice joined him at his gesture of invitation.

"I'm afraid we'll have to devise some other way of discovering the Master," he said heavily. "Whiting will have to go free, of course."

Kirkpatrick nodded gravely, but Colonel Rice set his lips in disapproval. "Only way to win this war," he said, "is to kill them off from the top. At least hold them as hostages."

Wentworth's brain gave an involuntary assent to Rice's words but it was a policy to which he could not subscribe. This fight could be won only by the destruction of the Master. As long as he lived, he could find fresh puppets to do his bidding. Whiting was no more than that….

"Bring in Miller," Wentworth directed Jackson.

A few moments later, a stocky, square-shouldered man was led in, blindfolded. He seemed in no way incommoded by not being able to see. He stepped out with a strong confidence that showed his courage and his solid lips had a quiet smile.

"I've come a devilish long and inconvenient way to see you, Wentworth," he said. "I hope I am going to see you?"

"Of course," Wentworth agreed and, at his gesture, the blindfold was removed.

His steady gray-blue eyes studied the face that was revealed. It was square and determined, the brows horizontal above direct blue eyes. As soon as he was again accustomed to the light, Miller unbuttoned his vest and, from an inner pocket, produced his credentials.

"You'll want to see these, of course," he said, "but I think my message will convince you more than the papers. The President has arranged for an election to be held ten days from tomorrow in the form of a recall election on Governor Whiting. It is conditional on your surrendering Governor Whiting into my hands for immediate return to Albany!"

RELEASE OF Governor Whiting accorded well with Wentworth's plans. Nothing was to be gained by his longer incarceration since there seemed no doubt that he knew nothing of the Master's identity. In himself, the man was unimportant. His destruction might merely allow another, actively criminal, man to take his place. So, when Wentworth had satisfied himself of the authenticity of the credentials submitted by Miller, he allowed him to depart with Governor Whiting, blindfolded as they had come.

Instantly, Wentworth began to organize his election campaign. Ten days allowed little enough time, but there could be no question that the bulk of the people were hostile to Whiting. Their opinions did not need to be swayed—what was needed was the mass courage to vote their convictions. And instilling the necessary strength into the electorate was an even bigger task. More than any other single thing, the capture of the Master would help, but months of work had failed to uncover him. There was small hope that the next ten days would be much more fruitful.

Wentworth must send his men everywhere to encourage the people, to fight against the tyrannies of the Black Police and give the voters at least the illusion of protection. Against one thing, however, Wentworth was powerless—the plague. Of those among his followers who had been stricken, only the ones who had received the injection showed any improvement. The others were dying by a slow process of living disintegration. If they failed at the polls, it would be the plague which defeated them!

The victims were everywhere. In little abject bands they roamed the countryside with the placards ordered by the state placed upon their backs, with small mournful bells jangling constantly to their shuffling walk. If the mass of the people believed that the plague fought on the side of the criminals— that to oppose the Black Police was sufficient to bring on the plague—Wentworth's task became practically impossible. Against that, his only weapon could be the free dispensing of the anti-plague injections. Therefore he organized a series of raids on various scattered hospitals.

The task Wentworth had chosen for himself was at once the most important and most dangerous. With swift skill, he assembled a powerful portable radio broadcaster and set out on a tour of the state. He had to make brief, pungent speeches, while the radio car sped along the road, but his talks could run for but a few minutes only. Well he knew that the Black Police would be listening in and, by means of swiftly organized triangulation, locate his position. Thus it was speak, then flight across the back roads and presently speak again from a position fifty miles away.

Twice the racing cars of the Black Police converged so rapidly that he escaped only after a running gunfight After that, Kirkpatrick insisted on organizing a guard under Colonel Rice—a half dozen armed men in an enclosed truck which would pace the radio car. To Wentworth this seemed a mistake because it hampered mobility and increased the likelihood of attracting suspicion. However, on the insistence of his men, he gave in.

The radio work must not stop, for the whispers of menace from the plague spread daily. Wherever the men of the Spider gained some transient advantage, the plague was sure to strike more terribly than ever. The fears of the people were so increased that, twice, the Spider's men had been driven from towns. The citizens preferred to submit to tyrannies and robberies rather than face the certainty of the plague!

It was on the second day after Wentworth accepted a guard, and a bare three days before the election, that the Spider had actually to force himself to make his daily patrol in the radio car. He had an overwhelming sense of disaster—a curious coldness in his breast that he recognized from many similar experiences. It was the warning of his subconscious against danger. He paid it no heed other than to ask of Colonel Rice special alertness.

"Call it a hunch," Wentworth said somberly, "perhaps only a

feeling of depression of spirits because things have been going so badly for us. I find it wise not to ignore hunches."

Colonel Rice nodded his blunt head and his eyes were anxious. "I've been worried, too. Perhaps it would be better not to go today."

Wentworth's lips closed grimly. "If we relax the fight, we lose what small chance of victory we have. I'm laying plans for a raid that I hope may turn the tables. We'll talk it over tonight."

THE ROADS over which Wentworth sped that day were strangely deserted. Not once in an hour did they pass another machine. In the towns, too, few persons were in sight, save for the melancholy bands of the plague-stricken. The sight of them shook Wentworth with a helpless fury. The Master and the Black Police had turned back civilization a thousand years!

As the car left the limits of the town, Wentworth began to speak. Beside him, his driver kept a sharp outlook. He was a young chap named Forrester whose father had been murdered by the Black Police and Wentworth had chosen him deliberately for his skill—and his loyalty. As Wentworth finished his speech, Forrester jerked his head angrily.

"These empty roads have got me worried," he muttered. "Looks almost as if they were barricaded—even if we ain't found any yet."

The words had scarcely left his lips when the trumpet horn of the patrol truck, which had rounded a curve ahead, rang out in a triple-blast which signaled an attack! Before its last note had sounded, machine guns began to hammer.

Forrester slammed on brakes. "A barricade!" he snapped.

"Go on!" Wentworth ordered. "That truck should be able to smash through!"

The car picked up speed again, eased around the curve—and the truck was motionless in the road. Guns crashed out from its loopholes, but none of the men who manned the auto barricade fell under that fire. The attackers leaped out with their guns in their hands and, with a soft oath, Wentworth guessed the reason for that ineffective fire! These were not the Black Police, but National Guardsmen in khaki! Colonel Rice could not bring himself to fire on them!

Well, that was in accordance with Wentworth's desires, too. Never, even at the risk of his life, had he hurt innocent men and, though these guardsmen fought the battle of the Master, they were only obeying orders from the governor as they were sworn to do....

"Back!" Wentworth ordered.

Forrester was already fighting the car around. Bullets began to slam against the car. Wentworth twisted about and stared down the road behind. Side by side, two trucks filled with men in khaki, were trundling up the road. That way, too, was blocked! Desperately, Wentworth's eyes searched the woods that crowded the road. On one side, the hill climbed steeply; on the other, a sharp declivity dipped toward a valley, but the trees were thinner.

Steadily, Wentworth ordered Forrester to drive from the road and attempt to thread a way through the trees. The driver nodded with quick comprehension, his eyes sharp and eager. The car lurched across the ditch, smashed through a fringe of underbrush and rocketed down the slope. A stump blocked their path, and Forrester swerved around it, scraped off a fender against a tree—but roared on.

Wentworth's eyes swept the way ahead. By following a zigzag path, there seemed every chance that they would manage to make the open field below the woods. A half mile away was a farmhouse, and there would be a road there to the highway beyond. Hope began to rise again in Wentworth's breast. He peered behind. The troops had been thrown from the trucks and were lined up for volley fire, their rifles snouting perilously down the steep grade.

"Down!" Wentworth snapped to Forrester. "Stop and duck!"

Instead, Forrester wrenched the wheel violently. The car made a skidding turn around a thick-boled maple, turned again and drove down the grade... and the rifles crashed out in a single, heavy concussion of volley fire. The windshield dissolved in slashing, silvery fragments. Forrester uttered a choked cry and was driven forward across the wheel, slain instantly. By some miracle unhurt, Wentworth made a frantic grab for the wheel. Too late. The car, like a thing possessed, hurled itself squarely against a tree!

Wentworth felt himself plucked from his seat by the giant's hand of momentum and pitched through the air. He had a whirling glimpse of barren tree limbs overhead, then dazzling light and utter blackness struck him in one agonizing blow.

As his senses flickered and went out, he had a single despairing thought. If he were not killed, he would be captured—and the Black Police would see to it that, if he regained consciousness at all, it would be only to dangle at the end of a rope! This was the end—and that end was triumph for the Master!

CHAPTER 7
VOTES FOR MURDER!

THERE WAS no need for outlaw spies to carry the word of disaster to the Catskill camp or to Nita in her hideout in New York City. Within a half hour of Wentworth's capture, unhurt except for superficial lacerations and a concussion, the news was broadcast from every state-controlled radio. They calculated on the effect of that announcement to smash the final opposition to Governor Whiting and turn the election overwhelmingly in his favor—the election that was only three days away....

But the Master was not content with that. Wentworth was ordered, as the Spider, to immediate trial in Albany on multiple charges of murder. The radio carried more announcements that members of Wentworth's band had confessed their complicity and his; that many of the Black Police were in his pay; and that Wentworth and Wentworth alone was responsible for the spread of the plague. His men had stolen experimental virus from the hospitals, it was charged, and, under the guise of administering antitoxin, had infected fresh hundreds with the dread White-Face Plague!

Such a trial could have only one end and Nita, hearing the news in her New York City hideout, was brought, pale-faced and terrified, to her feet.

Her impulse was to dash madly to Albany to Wentworth's side to share whatever fate was to be his, but she fought down that madness. She must play a much more desperate role than that. She must fly to the Catskill camp and help organize Wentworth's rescue. Kirkpatrick would be there, but such furtive attempts were not his strong point. No one could be better at leading men, or in an open attack, but no such means would succeed in this case. The Black Police would be ready for a frontal attack.

Within a few minutes after the announcement had come over the air, Nita was in action. She recalled Sailor Joe and Ram Singh from the tasks to which they had been assigned and laid her plan before them.

"You two will put on Black Police uniforms," Nita ordered, "and commandeer a plane to fly me, as a prisoner, to Albany. We must get there at once before any foolish frontal attack is organized and our man-power wasted."

Ram Singh drew himself to his full, powerful height. *"Wah, missie sahib,"* he cried. "I will myself fly to Albany. I will break into the governor's home and my knife…" His hand went to the heavy hilt, half-concealed at his waist.

"You will have your chance to use those knives!" Nita said and her voice was cold and fierce. "But tonight is not the time."

Sailor Joe tugged his forelock. "You're giving the orders, skipper. Me and Whiskers here will trail along."

Ram Singh's eyes flashed toward the broad-shouldered, red-faced man, but he recognized that no affront had been offered to his dignity. They had fought side by side before this! He bowed to Nita, cupping his palms to his forehead.

"Yours to command, *missie sahib!*" he said, gutturally. "There is a thing I have learned today, *missie sahib*. All the supplies of anti-toxin for the plague are being brought to New York City and placed under heavy guard in the Sixty-Ninth Regiment Armory. It is to stop the raids of our men."

Nita nodded, scarcely conscious of what the Sikh said. Dick needed her help. That was her only thought now. "Hurry!" she ordered. "The Black Police uniforms!"

She kneeled and opened a secret section of the baseboard and removed the uniforms, tossed them at the men. She drew out also some forged official forms such as the Black Police used and skillfully, with her hand trained in drawing and painting, forged a warrant for herself and an order to commandeer an airplane. When she had finished, Sailor Joe and Ram Singh strode back into the room.

"I keep telling him he ought to shave off them whiskers," Sailor Joe said. "They'll spot us sure."

· *NITA VAN SLOAN* ·

Nita smiled. "Sikhs never shave," she said quietly. "It is a part of their religion...."

Ram Singh said harshly, "Yours to order, *missie sahib*. If these miserable hairs endanger you and the master, they shall come off!"

Nita shook her head, though tears touched her eyes. She realized the sacrifice Ram Singh offered to the cause. In his own eyes, he would be eternally disgraced if he removed his beard, shorn of his birthright as a Singh, a lion of warriors. "If you have escaped detection in New York City in the work you have been doing," she said, "you'll be safe enough tonight. Come, we must hurry!"

The papers Nita had forged got them their plane and, within the hour, they were in the air and speeding toward the Catskill camp. The flight was brief and, presently they slanted to a landing in a pasture. The plane was rapidly wheeled into the cover of the woods and a car, hidden for that purpose in a near-by deserted barn, sped them on their way to the camp. They switched presently to horses and, after what seemed to Nita an interminable time, the hails of sentries stopped them, then heralded them to the camp.

Nita was stricken afresh by the camp. Usually, there was a supporting buoyancy, a brisk and hopeful tone to the very voices of the men. Today, there was a forlorn and despairing droop to men's shoulders. Their challenges and cries were listless. Overhead, the skies were leaden and seemed to sag to the very hilltops. As Nita entered the stockade before the tree-masked cabins, a cold rain began to lash downward. The wind made a deep mourning in the barren trees.

NITA FOUND the main cabin packed with fully fifty men and, standing on a chair at one end, was Kirkpatrick addressing them. "Our spies," he was saying, "have brought us word that tonight, the commander will be held in the Black Hole concentration camp and taken some time during the night or tomorrow morning to Albany for trial. That is our chance…" He broke off at sight of Nita, stepped down to greet her.

Kirkpatrick's lean face had grown more dour and drawn since last she had seen him. In his eyes, too, there was hopelessness— as if he knew in advance that what he proposed was foredoomed to fail.

The men were all staring at her, Nita realized, and they even raised a muffled cheer. It was not that they distrusted Kirkpatrick, but all their loyalty was given to Wentworth. It was the reflection of that whole-hearted service to the Spider which made them turn to Nita now. It was a weapon she could use to forestall the madness of the thing Kirkpatrick was planning. It was plain that he had no specific information as to time and route, or even the method by which Wentworth would be taken to Albany. Their strength was too slight to risk on so long a chance.

"I bring a message from Dick," Nita told Kirkpatrick, her voice low, but her eyes direct as she told the lie. "One of my spies managed to get near him."

Kirkpatrick's face brightened. "Splendid!" he cried and swung to the men. "Miss van Sloan brings a message from the commander!"

Nita's conscience troubled her at the way in which her lie was whole-heartedly accepted. She was lifted to the chair where a moment before Kirkpatrick had stood.

"The commander says," Nita's voice rang clearly, "to carry on the election campaign! He has a plan for his own release and

111

the capture of the Master! He will communicate when the time is ripe!"

There was nothing half-hearted about the cheer that was raised this time. Harassment left their faces as if by magic and Nita put a gay smile on her own lips.

"I'm not sure," she said lightly, "but it almost seems that the commander intended himself to be captured, but wouldn't tell you about it because he knew you would not want him to run that risk for you. He says, 'Keep on fighting!' He says, 'Our day is near!' He says, 'I will send you word!' Dismiss and spread the message!"

The men trooped out and, when they were gone, Nita's shoulders drooped in spite of her strongest efforts. Kirkpatrick hurried toward her eagerly. From a distant corner of the room, a small man in a priest's black robe came toward her. He had a rueful smile on his gentle face.

"It was gallantly done, daughter," he said, "but why need you lie to these men?"

Nita held out her hands to the priest, "Father Flower!" she cried gladly. "You can ask that? Didn't you see how much stronger they were! How much more bravely they went out!"

Kirkpatrick's face was dazed. "You lied?" he repeated. "You… lied? Then Dick has no plan? What madness is this, Nita?"

Nita spun on him. "It is madness to make an attempt to save Dick when you don't know the plans! How do you know they won't fly Dick to Albany, and send out a machine-gun company in trucks to trap you! We have too few men to risk them that way with Dick's life, and the fate of the whole state in the balance!"

For a moment, stern anger darkened Kirkpatrick's face, but slowly it faded. "You are right," he said, almost humbly. "If you who love Dick so dare to wait, then it is not for me to order immediate action. Do you have any plan?"

"Only one," Nita said quietly. "Wait—and send spies to learn the truth. Our best chance will come during the trial in Albany. When that day comes, Stanley, one of us must wear the robes of the Spider. In a fair court, that might convince them that Dick was not guilty. Aside from that, with the Spider to lead them—and remember that the men know Dick is only using the Spider's identity and name to strengthen the cause—the men will fight each with a dozen men's strength."

Kirkpatrick's face was pale, but there was fierceness in his clear blue eyes. "That will be my job," he said softly. "It is only right that I should wear the robes of the Spider—I who have fought him so many times and with such a sore heart. Perhaps, in that way, I can make amends." His voice was desperate, but forlorn. It was as if he pledged himself to a cause lost before it was launched.

But Nita knew how great an effort that declaration cost him. Even in the battles as an outlaw, Kirkpatrick had done his best to uphold the law and order to which he had given a lifetime of service. If he were discovered in the Spider's robes, not even the eventual triumph over the Master, the complete cleansing of the state, could ever restore him to his previous position. And yet, he was the man to lead!

Nita said quietly, "I agree."

Father Flower sighed, "I shall pray!"

He moved away to his room, and Kirkpatrick led Nita to the blazing fireplace. "Nita," he said slowly, "there was a hidden significance in your words that perhaps you didn't recognize yourself. You said that Dick had planned for himself to be captured. I've been afraid from the first of something close to that—that some of our own men planned it for him!"

"You mean… treachery!" Nita gasped. "Oh, no, none of these men would do that to Dick. They are too loyal!"

"Colonel Rice commanded the guard," Kirkpatrick said slowly. "The truck was rolling ahead and the road was blocked only by a barricade of cars. He could have rammed them aside. He didn't even try. He had machine guns but the attacking men suffered not a single casualty of any kind!"

"But Colonel Rice is being put on trial with Dick!" Nita cried. "Surely, he wouldn't do such a thing as that!"

Kirkpatrick shook his angular head bitterly. "I have been debating the possibility that Colonel Rice is the Master himself!" he said. "We know that it must be some one who has access to the Capitol. Rice has it. We know that once before the Master hid behind the identity of a minor official. He posed as the governor's secretary!"

"You may be right," Nita said slowly, "but if that's so, then the Master knows all the secrets of our camp! He may be, at this very moment, surrounding us here!"

Like an echo to her words, guns crashed suddenly outside the cabin and men shouted an alarm. A machine-gun chattered in a long, furious drum roll. Kirkpatrick and Nita stared at each other, then Kirkpatrick snatched his revolver from an under-arm holster and raced for the door.

"If we're attacked in force," he called back over his shoulder. "There's only one thing to do! We'll have to slip out by the crawl-way Dick arranged. It's our only chance!"

Even as he reached the door, there was a stunning blast and through its rumbling concussion, Nita heard the screams of a man and the roar of an airplane engine. Other explosions followed sharply on the heels of the first.

"We must retreat at once!" Nita called. "There's no time to delay. It does not matter how few men are outside, the camp has been discovered now and is useless!"

Kirkpatrick nodded brusquely, stepped outside the door. Nita heard his voice lifted in command and she ran to the trapdoor which opened into the basement beneath the cabin—and the crawlway which had been built by the idle men stationed here in the months of the Master's domination. It had been finished before Colonel Rice came to the camp, and there was a strong likelihood that he had not been told about it. If he had—Nita's lips twisted—then everything was lost, and Dick would never be rescued unless he could devise means to free himself!

Men began trooping into the cabin. Sailor Joe and Ram Singh hurried toward her, bringing Father Flower. "We got orders to take you out first, Miss Nita," Sailor Joe said hoarsely, "and we ain't got much time. Captain Kirkpatrick is going to blow up everything when the last man is through."

Nita drew in a slow, deep breath. Treachery and defeat, Dick a captive… They were beaten now, finally, permanently. She threw back her head and laughed, "Now, we begin to fight!" she cried. "I'll lead the way!" She went down in the darkness and damp gloom of the basement and moved toward the masked entrance of the crawlway....

RICHARD WENTWORTH learned of the disaster at the camp during the first day of his trial when the prosecutor made his opening address before the court.

"We are happy to announce," said the prosecutor, "that the last encampment of the outlaws has been annihilated. Men captured with the prisoner before the bar were glad to confess in greatest detail and to tell the secret of the camp where they had been virtually enslaved...."

Wentworth knew the helpless burn of fury. He had heard the evidence of those men who were "glad to confess." He had been a helpless prisoner in a dark, tiny cell at the main concentration camp when that had happened. He had heard the screams of men under torture. He could not blame them. Pain could loosen almost any tongue. His attention was drawn sharply to the prosecutor.

"We deliberately waited to allow them time to call in their reserves scattered all over the state," the man was saying. "Three flew in from New York City, two of them traitorously disguised as Black Police and bringing a woman with them who, we are reliably informed, is the inamorata of the prisoner before the bar. They were destroyed, all of them, in the attack!"

Wentworth found himself dazedly on his feet, felt the hard grip of hands upon his arms that dragged him to his chair again. But he scarcely heard the order that caused him to be chained down. Nita… Nita had flown to the camp and been… God, no, that couldn't happen to brave Nita!

So he consciously told himself, but there was a cold despair that told him this was truth. It was precisely what Nita would have done when she learned of his capture. She would have sped to the camp to organize rescue. If the blow had been intended to destroy Wentworth's morale, it had succeeded terribly. His spirit was not broken, but there was in him no will to live. Even if he escaped now, it would be a single-handed contest against overwhelming force. Kirkpatrick, Nita… gone.

During that day, he scarcely heard the procession of glib witnesses who confessed that they had helped Wentworth in his efforts to rob the state and put the blame upon the regularly elected officials. This was a cleverer plan than the Soviet government had thought out. Instead of permitting intimidated men to testify, they sent substitutes to court under the names of the accused. But when sentence was passed, it would be Wentworth's allies who were executed! On the stand, they confessed, too, that they had deliberately spread the plague through the state, under the guise of administering anti-toxin!

When the long day was finished, the eve of election, Wentworth was led, still in chains, back across the armored bridge that had been built to connect with the jail. Through a high, bullet-proof window, he caught a glimpse of the street. It was filled with troops for two blocks around. Barricades fronted the jail building and the court and there were mounted machine guns upon it. Bewilderment touched Wentworth. If the last band of his men had been wiped out, why were all these precautions being taken against rescue? For a moment, he knew a gleam of hope, but it died quickly. It must all be intended merely to impress upon the people that revolt was useless.

One of the guards jostled him away from the window and sneered at him, "We're protecting you against the mob," he said hoarsely. "After they found out you spread the plague, they wanted to lynch you. We wouldn't want nothing like that to happen to you."

Only once during the election day, the second and last day of the Wentworth's trial, did he rouse from his lethargy. That was when Miller, the G-man who had taken Governor Whiting back to Albany from the Catskill camp made a brief appearance in court.

"This trial is completely irregular!" Miller shouted at the judge, his square face an angry red. "The prisoner has been given no chance to prepare his defense! I warn you that the federal government will take action!"

Miller was expelled from the court, and there were no further interruptions to the glib steadiness of the "confessions" that condemned him. The jury returned its verdict without leaving the box and the spectacled judge leaned toward Wentworth. He had been a political magistrate in New York City when the Whiting regime had begun but deaths and "resignations" had opened the way to the higher bench. He smiled thinly now.

"Does the prisoner have anything to say before sentence is passed upon him?" he asked and the question was like a threat.

Wentworth pushed heavily to his feet under the weight of his chains. Now that the travesty was ended, he found the remnants of his courage again. His head came up and the twist of his lips was mocking as of old. His friends were gone, his allies smashed, but he was still alive. He had begun his battles against the underworld alone long ago. Bereft of friends, he would be stronger than ever, because no longer were there any ties to hold him back.

"I'm afraid," he said dryly, "that truth would carry no weight in this court. Go ahead and sentence me, you hireling of crooks. God knows what name you put to the proceedings here, but they are a mockery to the name of justice!"

The judge's face turned angrily red, and a guard's fist smashed Wentworth back into his chair.

"Stand!" the judge shouted. "Stand while you are sentenced!"

Wentworth's bloodied lips still held their mocking smile as he pushed to his feet again. "That was well done," he said, "and typical of this court's justice!"

"Silence!" The judge was on his feet now. "Richard Wentworth, I sentence you to die by whatever means the state has decreed for the death of traitors! You will die tomorrow at sunrise!"

Wentworth started at the pronouncement. He had known he would be executed, but so soon! He flung back his head and clung to his smile. He was not yet dead!

"With you will die," the judge shouted on, "the nine men who have confessed you as their leader, in murder and crime!"

Wentworth's eyes swung toward the nine smiling men who had posed as his adherents and "confessed." Well, they knew that the men whose names they bore would die in their stead! Fury shook off every shred of Wentworth's despair. By God, somehow, he would break free and smash this corruption....

"Take the prisoner away, and do justice upon him!" the judge finished hoarsely.

As the guards gripped Wentworth's shoulders and thrust him once more toward the armored bridge that led to the jail and his double-barred cell, the prosecutor rose suavely to his feet.

"Thank you, your honor," he said pleasantly. "This completes our victory. I'm sure you will be glad to know, your honor, that the vote in the election today was ninety-eight percent for Governor Whiting. Next election, I think the other two percent will swing into line, too. It will be healthier!"

The court attendants broke into uproarious laughter and that was the sound that rang in Wentworth's ears as he was thrust into his cell, and the five men of the death watch took their stand outside. The chains were still on his ankles and wrists.

CHAPTER 8
EXECUTION DAWN

HELPLESS IN his chains, Wentworth sat out the long hours of the night. It was hard to cling to courage when the end was so near and so certain. He long ago had tested the strength of his tool-steel chains and found them beyond his strength. Under the constant vigilance of the five guards, there was certainly no hope. He tried to shape some plans. Would the execution take place here? Wentworth thought not. The nine men sentenced to die with him were still at the main concentration camp so far as he knew. If that were so, he would be moved some time during the night to the camp, or they would be brought here....

Wentworth schooled himself in patience to wait for that. Ten men were to be executed together. Even weighted with chains, ten men were a force to contend with. If he could stir them to action... It was past midnight when a file of men tramped down the hall and his cell door was thrown open. Without words, Wentworth was chained between two of the Black Police who formed the guard and marched along echoing corridors.

Other prisoners sprang from their bunks to stare at him with white faces. They cursed him, heaped abuse upon his head. "The Plague-Bringer," they called him and the bitter words twisted a dull knife in Wentworth's heart. Even if he won freedom, what could he hope to accomplish against such madness as this? The people blaming him, fighting instead of helping him! He could look for no further action from Washington, since the election had failed. Before long, the Master might be stretching out his tentacles toward the nation's capitol itself!

Wentworth's thoughts were broken off short as he saw the arrangements that had been made for transporting him. An armored truck, such as was used to transport money, had been converted into a prison truck. He was wedged into a metal-lined cell barely large enough to receive him, the door slammed and locked. All around him was the roar of truck and motor-cycle motors, and he had glimpsed machine guns mounted on them all.

Once more a transient doubt touched Wentworth. Were all

these precautions really necessary to guard against his being lynched? Or had the prosecutor lied about the complete destruction of his forces? The memory of the curses of the other prisoners came back to Wentworth and he deliberately killed his hope. No, escape must rest with him alone.

The truck lurched forward finally and, amid the clattering of a score of exhausts, got under way. Hours dragged past. It was only by a rigid exercise of his utmost will power that Wentworth resisted the inclination to fight against the close-pressing steel walls. They seemed to be strangling him, squeezing out his life. He controlled himself, but the effort left him exhausted. His knees sagged, but he could not even sit between the coffin-close walls.

The tapping must have been going on for minutes before Wentworth was even conscious of hearing it. He strained his ears then and caught, vibrating through the steel, a rhythmic series of barely audible sounds. Then he recognized Morse code and his heart leaped with hope—to die at once. It could not be any one except another prisoner. Nevertheless, when the Morse tapping stopped signaling his name, Wentworth caught up a link of steel and began to rasp out an answer.

"Who are you?" he signaled.

The reply came back deliberately. *"Miller. Sentenced to camp. Is there any chance of rescue?"*

Wentworth smiled wryly in the darkness. Did Miller also think him a miracle man? *"None,"* he tapped back. *"None at all."* He hesitated a moment then asked the question which had been gnawing at his heart for days, *"Was my camp really destroyed?"*

Miller answered with a single word, *"Yes!"*

So that faint hope was finished! Miller proceeded to tap out some of the details about the attack, about the election. Every word that clicked out of the steel seemed to drive despair deeper into Wentworth's soul. His control snapped and for a moment, he fought wildly against the steel walls. His chains clattered, nearly deafened him in that narrow space. Finally, he sagged exhausted.

IT WAS perhaps an hour afterward that a series of hails signalized their entrance into the concentration camp. Hauled finally from his cell, Wentworth found himself scarcely able to walk, but he was hustled along without mercy. He saw that the east was faintly gray. Dawn. Execution dawn. Was it so close then to the time when he was to die?

Wentworth threw back his head and sucked the crisp, cold air into his lungs. Overhead the autumn sky was purple with increasing light. The ground was iron hard with frost and rang under his heels. The shackles were burning cold against the bare flesh of his wrists. Wentworth stared hungrily about him. It was this hunger for life within him which convinced him that he had not given up hope—not consciously. He would fight before he died, but what could it accomplish?

Men were stirring this early in the day. He could make out faintly the blockhouses on the quadruple walls and fences that ringed the camp. Over there near the guardhouse… Wentworth stared. It was a priest, all right, but it couldn't possibly be Father Flower! The next instant, Wentworth strangled his hopes again.

Even if it were the gentle priest of the outlaws, it could mean nothing except that he had come to offer final consolation.

Wentworth was on the point of asking for the priest, but restrained himself. So long as he did not talk with the man, he might in his secret heart hope that Nita had escaped the camp. It could not be Father Flower, of course....

Wentworth was hustled roughly across the quadrangle and thrust once more into a cell. At the sound of his entrance, other men stirred in their cells and pushed their pale faces against the bars. Wentworth realized that he was once more among his men, those who had been condemned without even the travesty of a trial—doomed by men who used their names and lyingly confessed. At sight of him, they broke into a subdued cheer.

"The commander is back, men!" one cried softly. "Now we'll rip open this sardine can!"

Even in this moment of extremity, they counted on him! They could have faith that he would once more work one of those miracles which, time after time, had snatched them and himself from death. How vain it was now! Wentworth opened his lips to tell them so—and could not. Let them hope. It would give them courage to the end. Let them even think he had a plan....

"Wait for my command," he whispered, "then strike! One of you ask for a priest!"

It had been an inspiration, that last. Let them think, too, that there was some chance of help from outside. Perhaps it was not vain. If they would all attack at his command, some might fight their way clear... Before the thoughts had coursed through his brain, armed guards were marching once more down the corridor. The cells were opened one by one and each man, as he was led out, had a steel collar locked about his neck—a collar whose chain linked him inescapably, before and after, to his companions. Their hands remained chained before them and short links coupled their ankles together.

Wentworth strangled down a mad impulse to wild laughter. Fight! Fight in chains that way? He stared despairingly at the faces of the men, but they were not downcast. There was in them instead a grim determination. One or two looked toward him, and there was a sly humor in their eyes, mingled with an almost idolatrous worship. Because he had bid them hope, not even these chains could daunt them.

WENTWORTH GRIPPED the steel bars of his cell until his forearms burned with the pain of the tension. They counted on him. Could he let them down? By God, he would not somehow, before they were slaughtered, he would strike! It was his turn now. Men with drawn revolvers stood outside his cell and two men came in together with the last collar of the chain. It was clamped strangling-tight about his throat. Outside, he could hear one of the men pleading for a priest, babbling, begging....

"How are we to die?" Wentworth asked quietly. "The court did not say."

The leader of the guard laughed hoarsely. "You'll find out soon enough. We got a neat new little gadget that ought to tickle your fancy."

One of the guards belched out a laugh. "Tickle his fancy! Gawd, that's good, chief! Tickle his fancy... Haw, haw, haw!"

There were guards at the head of the line and behind them

now. Wentworth eyed their guns hungrily, but his heavy-man-acled hands could not move swiftly enough to snatch one even if they came within reach. They had whips, too, and suddenly a lash bit through the clothing of his back and sent a stab of pain across his shoulders.

"March, you dogs!" the captain of the guard ordered. "March along. We got to kill you before we get to eat!"

Up ahead, the whips were cracking viciously and a man was still begging for a priest. They trooped along the concrete corridor dragging their chains, strangling against the steel collars, and debouched abruptly out into the quadrangle. It was dimly alight now with the increasing dawn and there was a faint redness to the clouds in the east Sunrise. The prisoners of the camp were lined up in long lax ranks, their faces drawn and apathetic in the dim gray light. One group of men stood a little apart from the others. They seemed stronger, more alert than the others. Abruptly, with horror springing in his soul, Wentworth swung back to the other men. He saw suddenly why they seemed so pale, why their lines and their manner were so listless and dull. They, too, were under sentence of death. Every man among them had the plague!

The man ahead of Wentworth in the chained line sagged suddenly back and began to cry out brokenly, fighting the forward pull of the chain about his throat. Guards were on him instantly, slashing him with whips. He sagged to his knees.

"God, no!" he whimpered. "I don't want to die that way! Not that way!"

Wentworth stared ahead then and saw… how they were to

die. A shudder tore at his soul and a fierce hot anger surged over him. In a glance, he saw the whole mechanism.

There was an electric winch with a chain fastened about the drum… a chain that would be hooked to their own and would draw them inescapably forward into the death machine. It was a circlet of stout, glittering steel blades like the chopping knives of a corn-fodder machine. As the chain drew them into those knives, they would be slashed to mincemeat—reduced to *fragments* of men while they still lived. No wonder the man ahead of him, brave fellow that he was, had collapsed in horror!

Now, he was staggering to his feet again under the bite of the whips. "A priest," he whimpered. "For the love of God, *a priest?*"

His voice wailed over the quadrangle. Wentworth saw a stir among those lines of doomed plague victims, and then, marching toward them, he saw again the black-garbed priest A feeling of utter incredulity shook him. *It was Father Flower!* If he had escaped from the Catskill camp, anything was possible….

Father Flower's gentle voice rang out clearly. "Peace, my children," he called. "If these men must die, let them make their peace with God!"

ONE OF the guards whirled on the priest, and the whip lashed out. It licked about Father Flower's throat, and blood sprang in a thin, red trickle where the lash had cut. The violence of the blow threw Father Flower off balance a little, but the expression of his face did not change.

"For that, too, I forgive you," he said, still gently. "Let me go now to these poor men!"

A mutter stirred over the plague-ridden ranks as three tracks

The man who gripped the lever of the
winch staggered and fell backward!

rolled abruptly out from behind the barracks buildings and
leveled mounted machine guns at the prisoners. Father Flower
ignored it all and came steadily on. The man who had struck
him with the whip fell back, abashed, before the priest's unwav-
ering courage.

"To hell with it!" the guard captain swore. "Get on with it"
His whip swirled over the doomed men.

Father Flower's voice cracked out with a sharp anger. "Do you hope for mercy from God, you who show no mercy to others? Shall I call down the vengeance of heaven upon you, miserable sinner? Shall I curse the flesh from your bones and the fingers from your hands? Shall I curse the eyes from your sinner's face?"

The captain flinched before the barrage of the priest's suddenly stern voice. He looked about, but his men were quailing, too, and Father Flower marched on, his crucifix held before him.

The captain said, sullenly, "I guess it won't hurt none to let the priest mumble over them!"

Father Flower was moving along the line of men now, touching them with his hands. A man in uniform swung down from one of the machine-gun trucks, started toward them at a run.

"Stop that priest!" he shouted. "Get on with the execution!"

He caught up the end of the chain that was fastened to the winch in the slaughter machine. Dragging it forward, he fastened it with his own hands to the collar of the first man in the line.

"Start that winch!" he shouted.

Instantly, the slack of the chain was taken up and the slashing knives began to revolve. The sun pushed its red rim over the horizon, and its angry light fell upon the glistening blades, staining them as if already they were performing their butchery. The doomed men ahead of Wentworth braced themselves, fought frantically against that deathly chain, but their strength was not the equal of that machine-monster which dragged them to doom. Wentworth felt his own chain tighten and begin to drag him forward.

"Say the word, commander!" the man ahead of him pleaded. "Say the word, and let us strike now before it is too late!"

Father Flower was hurrying to keep pace with the line. He was abreast of Wentworth now, and Wentworth saw how pale his face was. His lips were moving in prayer. The first man was within a yard of those murderous, flashing knives!

"God help me," Father Flower was whispering. "God help me, I cannot permit this butchery! I…" Abruptly, his hand slid out of his robe and he held out a small, powerful revolver to Wentworth. "Do not kill, commander, unless you have to," he said. "It is my hand, which deals the bullets you fire!"

WENTWORTH'S WEIGHTED hands gripped the revolver as if it were his eternal salvation instead of the feeble thing it was. It might kill a few of these butchers, but no more. At least, they could go out fighting like men, not slaughtered like cattle! A guard saw the revolver and shrieked a warning, whirled his whip over Father Flower's head. Wentworth squeezed off a shot. His heavily weighted hands did not matter now. He had no need to aim. The guard pitched backward to the earth… but Wentworth had heeded the word of Father Flower and had not killed.

He fired again, and the man who gripped the lever of the winch staggered and fell backward. He clutched at the lever as he fell, and the clattering of the winch stopped suddenly as the first man in the line pitched forward into the very maw of the knives.

"Free yourself from that chain!" Wentworth cried. "And strike! Seize their weapons! Turn them on the guard, on the machine guns!"

The little revolver was cracking again in his hand. Ahead of him in line, the whip-lashed man surged sideways and dragged Wentworth and the man ahead of him along. He got the guard's revolver.

"Flat on your faces!" Wentworth ordered. "Down for your lives!" With a sweep of his arm, he hurled Father Flower to the ground. Not an instant too soon! The machine guns burst into angry, hungry mirth.

"You prisoners!" Wentworth shouted at the plague-ridden men. "Do you love life so well? You are doomed anyway—dying! Kill some of the men who doomed you, before you die! Tear them to pieces with your hands. If you escape, I will cleanse you! I will cure your disease! It is the Spider who commands you! Fight!"

Like an echo of his words, guns began to hammer in the distance. There was the blast of a hand grenade, and he saw a machine-gun tower on the fence sag, riddled with the bursting shell fragments. Its gun was still.

"Help is coming!" Wentworth shouted. "My men are storming the walls! Fight, you dying men!"

It was a mad scene, a thing out of an insane man's dream. Men with palsied, disease ridden-hands. Men without fingers and limping on the stubs of their feet, turned in sudden wrath on the guards about them. The machine guns stammered, and they fell in windrows of death, but even those who were wounded rose and shambled on to attack their murderers. And outside, guns hammered and there were more grenades. Wentworth's gun clicked empty in his hand, but he crawled to where a guard had fallen and found another revolver, and ammunition.

With deliberate, deadly aim, he opened on the machine gunners in the armored truck.

He could aim now, and the Spider's steady guns hammered with the skill and steadiness of years of practice on range and on the battlefields of crime. One by one the machine guns fell silent.

"Open the gates!" Wentworth ordered. "Smash open the gates!"

A few, a score or two, plunged toward the gates. The others were mad with slaughter, with wreaking upon these fiends in black uniform the agony of months of oppression and imprisonment, with avenging their withering bodies, stricken by the malignancy of man-spread disease.

Through the bedlam of death, one voice rose in clear, sweet majesty and, even in the midst of battle, Wentworth turned his head in amazement.

On his knees, his face turned toward the burning sun that thrust now wholly above the horizon. Father Flower was praying... praying for the souls of the men who thus paid the penalty of their crimes! It was over, even while Father Flower prayed. The gates burst open and a tight little group of Wentworth's men, following a striding figure in the black robes of the Spider, dashed in to complete the seizure of the camp. And from the mouth of that man in Spider's garb came the crisp, ringing voice of... Stanley Kirkpatrick!

A great cry leaped from Wentworth's throat. He stumbled to his feet and his chained hands reached out—for, stumbling blindly forward, running toward him with her arms outstretched, was Nita!

CHAPTER 9
ARMY OF THE DYING

FOR A long moment, Wentworth gripped Nita's hands in his and his eyes blurred with tears, then her arms were locked tightly about his neck. Kirkpatrick's crisp voice was bringing order out of the chaos within the encampment. The last of the Black Police were being herded together, their machine-gun towers blown to bits. Even while he bent his head against Nita's fragrant hair, Wentworth's eyes were sweeping the enclosure.

There were many dead and dying upon the ground, but more than a thousand men were still on their feet. Most of them riddled with plague, yes, but frantic with hatred against the Black Police and the criminal overlord of the state. He had promised to cleanse them of their disease. By God, if they would follow him, he would! There were supplies of anti-toxin somewhere....

Now was the moment to strike—now while battle anger still shook them, while the state was rejoicing.

"Nita," he whispered. "Dear Nita... They told me you were dead!"

"Most of our camp were killed," Nita answered, her voice slow, heavy now with the relaxation of suspense. "A bomb collapsed the crawlway when only a few of us had broken through. But we gathered other men...."

"Do you know where there is a store of the anti-toxin?" Wentworth interrupted. "These men must have it."

Nita told him swiftly what she knew of the concentration of the stores in New York City to protect it from their raids.

"New York City," Wentworth whispered. "Why with that in our hands again..." He broke into sharp laughter. "Free me of these chains, Nita," he cried. "There should be keys at the belt of the captain of the guard. Free me of these chains—and we'll deliver New York City from the Black Police! Come on, hurry!"

Minutes later, freed of the chains, Wentworth sprang to the hood of a machine-gun truck. "Listen to me, you men who are dying!" he cried. "I will bring you life and vengeance at the same time! A chance to avenge your families—or to rescue those who still live! Will you follow me? In New York are all the stores of anti-toxin which the Black Police possess. They are off-guard. They think we are finished forever. Will you follow me, to strike again a blow for liberty and your own lives? Will you follow me—you men who are dying—and form an army of death!"

For moments after his strong voice had rung out against the walls of the prison barracks, there was silence. Then a shout rose. A hoarse, formless shout from the throats of men who had despaired, and now were given a glimpse of life. Wentworth had his answer—an army that would follow him to hell itself!

Before that red sun, which had risen to see men slaughtered, had lifted itself an hour above the horizon, the army of death was organized and ready. Captained by the few men whom Wentworth had trained, armed from the arsenals of the Black Police, and riding in prison vans and machine-gun armed trucks, the army of death was pouring toward New York City.

In a car that raced at their head, Wentworth laid his plans with Kirkpatrick. From him, he took the robes of the Spider and garbed himself in them. There was only one immediate cloud on the horizon, though it might well be that they rolled to their death. In all the prison, no one had been able to find a trace of G-man Miller.

"It's possible," Wentworth said slowly, "that they found he was signaling to me on the truck, and killed him. But I think not. Pass orders along the line that if G-man Miller is found, Kirk, he is to be brought to me. It is vitally important. Colonel Rice the Master, you say? No, he wasn't tried with me. And that is a little strange—*more* than a little."

Wentworth's gray-blue eyes stared emptily along the road ahead and, slowly, a smile began to tug at his lips. "I think," he said softly, "that I shall know the Master when I meet him! I think I shall know what to do!"

THE ARMY of death was rolling through Westchester now. In other days, there would have been a thick line of traffic, of men bound to offices in the cities. Today there were almost none. The state was dying, was almost dead. Unless they could rescue it soon… But today, they would wrest New York City from the Master, perhaps slay the Master himself!

Wentworth frowned. "Kirk, it's time to divide our force. You'll take a third of it and storm police headquarters. The radio will tell us when you have succeeded. There are two barracks of the

Black Police. Sailor Joe will lead against one of them, in the Bronx. I'll take the force against the down-town armory where the anti-toxin is stored."

He went on. "Once that is done, I'll go on the air, and appeal to the people. I think there will be small hesitancy on their part in deciding to help us, despite the propaganda of the Black Police and the Master against us. They couldn't really believe we would spread the plague. We have befriended too many of them!"

With those orders, Wentworth signaled a halt and the division of the forces was rapidly made. Father Flower, with Nita in the back of the car, was forlorn. It had been his hand, he felt, that had caused that slaughter in the city, and now more men were to die.

"It is the cause of heaven," he said, lifting his head now as the car was motionless. "If God had not intended it, he would not have let his servant prevail. I pray for you, Richard Wentworth."

Wentworth clasped the priest's hand warmly, "We'll try to deserve your prayers, father. Keep Nita safe with you."

Nita clung to Wentworth for a moment, then he was gone, striding to the car which would lead his contingent of the attack... Minutes later, the motorcade was under way again, but soon it divided and one line swung to the east behind Sailor Joe.

Presently, it divided again and Kirkpatrick parted with a swing of his hand. The cars filed past where Wentworth's column stood motionless and he saw the men's white, strained faces—the countenances of men who long had looked on death as their friend, and now hoped again. It was these men more than any

He moved up the stairs with the heavy machine gun kicking savagely in his arms!

other single factor, which would win the day. The Black Police would fight, but these men would be titans, without fear and without remorse.

WENTWORTH'S PLANS were fully laid for the attack upon the armory where the anti-toxin had been stored. He did not intend to expend the strength of his men in useless fighting through the streets of New York.

At the first intersection of his course with that of the East Side subway, Wentworth flung his men from their machines and down the kiosks. People saw the traces of the plague and fled in panic. The train, which stopped at the station, quickly emptied itself of passengers in the same way, and Wentworth's men took it over. The guards were imprisoned and a man with a gun in his hand stood beside the motorman. The train swung on to the express tracks and bored at top-speed down beneath the city.

When it was necessary to slow down because of trains ahead, they delayed short of the stations and went past them at top speed. How long it would be before the police learned of the seizure, Wentworth could not guess, but they would not know his destination—and the train made far better speed than the motorcade could possibly have achieved through the city streets.

He remained on the front car and strained his eyes ahead along the dim corridors of the subway. Station after station flashed past without an alarm. But it could not continue, Wentworth knew.

When the train reached the Thirty-third Street station, Wentworth abruptly halted it, disembarked his men and marched them at the double through crowds that parted hurriedly to give them passage. A squad of men, which Wentworth sent ahead, seized taxis on the street. And when his hundred and fifty men reached the surface, cars were waiting for most of them. Others were seized and, moments later, they were speeding southward again. Only a half dozen blocks to go now. Wentworth peered keenly ahead. As he watched, he saw a squad of Black Police dart from the entrance of the armory with a machine gun, and hurriedly set about rigging it up on a truck.

Calmly, Wentworth reached for the rifle of one of the men crowded into the cab behind him and took aim. At his first shot, a man was hurled bodily from the truck to the sidewalk. His second clipped the legs from under another policeman, and the balance bolted for the doors of the armory.

"On the sidewalk!" Wentworth snapped at his driver. "Right up the steps!"

The taxi hurdled the curb, bounced violently on the steps, but momentum carried them on. Just as the heavy metal doors were swinging shut, the taxi jammed in between, wedged them open. Wentworth was instantly out of the cab, revolver in each hand. He saw blurred, fugitive figures, and his guns spoke rhythmically. A rifle blasted close beside him and, up a flight of stairs, a man screamed. Wentworth whipped his head that way and, in the same instant, a grenade burst up there on the steps. There were more screams now. If that bomb had been thrown, the attack would have been blasted back in the same instant it began!

But more men were pouring past Wentworth now, coursing through the corridors with ready, hungry weapons, like hounds seeking a scent. Within two minutes, his entire force was within the armory. Wentworth ordered the taxi pushed out, the doors closed. Shots echoed from all sides within the building. Another bomb blasted, but the shouts that reached Wentworth's ears were cries of triumph... His men were winning out!

In fifteen minutes, the task was completed and the entire supply of anti-toxin, cases of it in an emergency-rigged refrigeration room, were in Wentworth's hands. Rapidly, he instructed a half dozen men in the use of the needle, left a hundred men on guard in the armory and, with fifty others, raced farther downtown in the confiscated taxis.

No doubt that a counter-attack would be launched shortly on the armory, but he had left ample men for its protection and they would be on the alert. Machine guns were mounted now in all the turrets and on the roof of the building, and hand-grenades distributed. Wentworth knew that, except for the surprise of his own offensive, he could not possibly have forced the building.

But the armory was a minor objective, for all that it gave him the ammunition to fight the plague. Unless police headquarters itself was seized, they could not hope to conquer the city. The mass of the regular police force must still be ready to back Kirkpatrick, Wentworth believed. Without a leader, cowed by the swift vengeance of the Black Police if they erred, they had worn the Master's harness. They would be glad to throw it off—if headquarters could be wrested from the crew that held it!

AS WENTWORTH sped southward through the city, the sounds of heavy gunfire came to his ears, punctuated by the heavier thud of grenades. His face whitened with anxiety. Plainly, the battle was being fought in the streets, for otherwise he would not have been able to hear the sounds so clearly. That meant Kirkpatrick had been ambushed! With the reserves the Black Police could command, a simple reinforcement of Kirkpatrick's line would not help. He must plan something....

Even as the thought flashed across his mind, a scream of sirens heralded a column of motorcycle Black Police. Just ahead of his own motorcade, they flashed across Fourth Avenue. Each machine carried two men, and in the sidecar a machine gun was mounted. No doubt for what purpose they were intended! They would take Kirkpatrick on the flank!

With the thought, Wentworth flung his men to the attack. He whipped up his revolver and, with deliberate shots, picked off the drivers of motorcycles.

Three times, Wentworth's rifle spoke just as a machine gun was being aligned and three times the operators were hurled, lifeless, from their rests. Guns crashed interminably from the cabs. Motorcycles, rammed by the charging cars, were crippled and their men fled in frantic haste. One taxi caught a burst from a machine gun and ran wildly up the street. It smashed two of the cycles before it rammed a brick wall and came to rest. Within it, nothing stirred at all, and Wentworth's rifle silenced the gun.

Swiftly then, Wentworth reorganized his men. Under the leadership of one of his outlaw lieutenants, he organized a motorcycle squad. It was to circle far to the east and come at the police headquarters from the rear.

"Cover every window in sight," Wentworth ordered sharply, "then send your men inside under the barrage. I think three men working together might get one of the motorcycles in through the side door. You could command the entire first floor from that point. I'll strike from the west."

A half dozen of the machine guns were wrested from the motorcycles and thrust into the taxis. They could be wedged in place in the windows in place of solid mounting. Their accuracy would not be high, but should be sufficient to cover a charge. Wentworth sprang back to the leading taxi again and sent it racing at top speed down the street. The hammer of gunfire was continuing. At least, they had not succeeded in wiping out Kirkpatrick's force yet....

Two blocks away from headquarters, Wentworth flashed past on his race to take the police center from the west and south. He saw cars blockaded across the street and men firing from behind and through them. He frowned. It didn't look good. Kirkpatrick had been compelled to set up a siege of the building. By means of radio and telephone, the Black Police could summon reinforcements to attack from the rear. The offensive had to be pressed home at once, or all was lost!

ABRUPTLY WENTWORTH halted the sweep of his cars, sent three men with messages to open the barricades. Then he divided his force into three parts, saving only three taxis, armed with machine guns, to go with him. Briefly, he outlined his plan.

"All three lines of cars will charge home at the same time," he directed. "Train your machine guns on the windows of police headquarters and race past, firing as fast as you can. You will all turn to the right when you hit Centre Street, and hug the right hand curb. I'm going to circle and come up Centre Street from the south. While your barrage is hammering at them, I'm going into the building."

Protests lifted from the men, but Wentworth silenced them with a wave of his arm. "Either we take that building in the next five minutes," he said quietly, "or the whole city is lost to us. That means death for all of us, of course, but it means much more. It means that we have lost all chance of ever reclaiming our state from these criminals! It means we are no longer free men, but slaves! It rests in your hands. Will you help?"

There was a rough, answering shout and the men raced back to their cabs. Wentworth, with his small force, tore off to the southward, cut across and back into Centre Street.

An instant later, the whole prospect opened up before him. At the door of police headquarters a dozen men's bodies lay sprawled, and they were the bodies of the attackers. Plainly, a machine gun had opened up from there on the instant when Kirkpatrick had thought victory within his grip. He had been forced to retreat behind barricades and attempt to shoot the Black Police out of their stronghold.

Flashes of gunfire came from the low-lying buildings opposite headquarters, and Wentworth realized snipers were at work there. It was good work. Eventually it would succeed, but there was no time to waste. Wentworth knew that the troop of motorcycle machine-gunners he had intercepted was only the first of many relief forces that would be soon dispatched. Once let them get inside the building....

His thoughts broke off as the first of the taxis, tires shrieking, cut into Centre Street. It was perfectly timed, for two other lines of taxis debouched from two other streets farther up at the same instant. Their guns opened as they entered the street and a heavy concentration of lead blasted out the windows of headquarters.

For a space of moments, while Wentworth's own force raced nearer and nearer, there was no response at all. Then from within the building, a machine gun opened up. The second taxi in line slewed wildly and charged straight across the street at the headquarters building itself. Its guns were silent and it struck the wall of the building with crushing force, bounced, trundled a few feet down the sidewalk and nuzzled the bodies that littered the doorway. A grenade lobbed into the street and wrecked a second taxi, blocked the race of the cars—but their barrage kept up. Bullets laid a solid sheet of metal against the windows.

Under that screaming arch of death, Wentworth drove his own attack home.

Now machine guns were opening in the side street also, from the captured motorcycles. Wentworth raced for the door, flung himself flat as a machine gun opened inside. Two of his men went down before that scything murder-stream, but the others dropped prone beside him and opened a heavy revolver fire.

Then a second machine-gun opened inside, farther back, and its lead did not scream out through the portal. The motorcycle attack had pressed home! With a shout and a wave of his arm to the men in the taxis, to Kirkpatrick's men at the barricades, Wentworth leaped for the doorway. A machine-gunner was dead across his barricaded weapon and, up the hall, a motorcycle was jammed half through a doorway, its machine gun commanding the approach.

FIERCELY, WENTWORTH caught up the machine gun of the slain Black Police. It was a heavy weapon, weighing seventy-five or eighty pounds, but in the fire of the attack Wentworth scarcely felt it. He moved toward the stairs with the gun kicking savagely in his arms.

There was a crouched squad of Black Police, a machine gun at the head of the steps. They scattered to the beat of Wentworth's bullets, were nailed screaming to the walls. Wentworth's men bounded up the stairs past him. Their shouts were hoarse with triumph.

There were screams of terror up there now as the disease-doomed men wreaked their vengeance on the Black Police whom they held accountable for all their misery. Wentworth dropped the hot machine gun, swung to others of the men pouring through the doors.

"Quickly!" he ordered. "Block the street with those taxis. Bring the machine guns in here and mount them on the first floor. Twenty of you take guns across the street and mount guns on the roofs of those buildings. Then let them try to drive us out of here!"

Wentworth sprang to the door. Kirkpatrick was already at work on the things he had just ordered and Wentworth laughed aloud at the sight. The armory was in their hands, and also police headquarters. If Sailor Joe had been able to drive home his attack in the Bronx....

"Quickly, Kirk!" Wentworth shouted. "Up to the radio room

and let your old command hear your voice! Those men are loyal to you, personally! A few words will do it and then…" Kirkpatrick was beside him, and they were mounting the stairs to the radio room.

"Then order them to arrest all the Black Police they sight! Tell them to shoot if there is an instant's resistance! Give us an hour and we'll have this city cleaned out and ready to resist any attack the governor may send against us!"

Kirkpatrick nodded curtly. "Thank God you came in time, Dick… Hell, man, where are you going now?"

Wentworth was already bounding back toward the stairs.

"I'm taking twenty men, Kirk!" Wentworth shouted back. "I think this is a good time to take charge of city hall! If you need more forces, draw on the armory for them!"

VOLUNTEERS FLOCKED to Wentworth at his call and he rapidly loaded them on a police emergency wagon and started a race toward city hall. As he swerved into Lafayette street, he flung on brakes frantically. From curb to curb the street was filled with marching people, thronging the way he was heading. Wentworth stared at them in amazement. Upon many were the ravages of disease and others bore the marks of torture at the hands of the Black Police. At their head… marched Nita and Father Flower, and the little priest bore aloft his crucifix.

It was a strange procession for a priest to lead and it was a strange song they sang. Wentworth caught the deep, hoarse vibrancy of its rhythm before he could identify its words or tune, and it swelled to the heavens, filled the canyons between the buildings.

THE SPIDER AT BAY

"Mine eyes have seen the Glory of the coming of the Lord,
He is trampling out the vintage where the grapes of wrath are
stored…."

Old men marched with their heads flung back in a rejuvenation of spirit that swept their years aside. There were women who carried children in their arms and boys who strode along blindly, gazing on a dream. One and all they chanted the glorious paean of a war fought eighty years ago for freedom.

With a curt command, Wentworth sent the emergency wagon circling back and presently it rolled with the van of the procession. Cheers broke their song at the sight of the Spider's black cape in their lead, the Spider marching beside the little priest with his up-raised crucifix—beside the woman who led them with her glorious voice.

It was madness and it was wonder. A squad of Black Police ranged out into their path and, with lifted guns, ordered a halt. If the people heard them, they did not heed. They marched on, singing, singing. From the emergency wagon, a blast of gunfire rolled out. A few of the Black Police fell, but the others fled. And Wentworth knew it was not the bullets that had driven them into flight. It was the spirit of those marching people whom not death itself could stop.

As they marched, other scores and hundreds poured into their flanks and buildings trembled to the tread of their march.

Now the city hall was in sight and, around it were lined deep ranks of Black Police. There were machine guns mounted behind barricades and armored cars loaded with rifle men. An officer on horseback galloped to meet the mob. His shouted words were

149

drowned out in the deeper thunder of people's singing voices. He yanked out a revolver and pointed it deliberately at Father Flower.

Wentworth's revolver spoke, and the man was hurled backward from the saddle. The people marched on.

Men were plucking up the priest now, catching hold of Wentworth, of Nita. Despite their violent efforts, they were passed back among the crowd, to safety from the threat of those guns. The marching people needed no leader now. The goal was in sight. Wentworth's shouted order to the men on the truck could not have been heard, but they, too, no longer needed a leader. Crowded behind the bullet-proof windshield of the truck, they opened fire. There were two Thompson submachine guns among them and, under the assault of bullets; men in black began to fall.

Now their machine guns, too, began to hammer. Swathes of blood were cut in those close-packed ranks, but they filled as soon as created, and never for an instant did the rolling chant of that battle hymn waver. The emergency truck crashed at full speed into the ranks of the Black Police. Many of them broke and fled, but others still hammered at the on-pressing thousands. They might as well have tried to stop the march of the waves, the hurricane blast of a tempest.

It was the sheer terror of the thing that could not be stopped— of men and women who marched singing to their certain death—that broke the spirit of the Black Police. Suddenly, the police were fleeing in every direction… and in no direction was there any escape. People fell upon them and slaughtered them with their bare hands, and all the while the song roared from their throats—the song of emancipation, of freedom and the triumph of the spirit over despair. The city hall was invested, overwhelmed.

Fighting to reach the mayor to force a surrender from him, Wentworth arrived minutes too late. He had been hanged from his own window by a score of willing hands.

WENTWORTH MOUNTED then to the window from which the body of the mayor dangled and managed at last to make his voice heard. A great waiting quiet fell upon the multitude while their white faces turned upward to the man in the window, their savior from oppression.

"Go to your homes now!" Wentworth called to them clearly. "Within three days an election will be held in which you shall name your new leaders! The police are in our hands. Anti-toxin against the plague will be distributed. Governor Whiting will be forced to resign. All will be well. Go home now. You have done your job!"

The cheer that went up from the square made windows tremble in their frames then slowly the fringes of the crowd began to break up.

He was heavy with weariness and shaken with doubts. He had promised that Whiting would be forced out, and that the state would be honestly ruled again, but God knew that was far from accomplished. If they had caught the Master, yes—but with him at liberty, the rest of the state might still be turned against them. The federal government might intervene to put down an armed rebellion, against a duly elected government. But if the Master were captured, the underlings would flee to cover, as the Black Police had scattered before the wrath of the aroused people.

Rapidly, then, Wentworth put through a phone call to police headquarters. "Victory here, Kirk," he reported steadily. "How did Sailor Joe fare in the Bronx?"

"Victory there, too," Kirkpatrick said briskly, "He has G-man Miller with him. Miller was locked up in a cell in the armory when Sailor Joe got in...."

Wentworth's voice leaped out. "Have a guard of fifty men thrown around Miller at once," he snapped, "and have him manacled hand and foot and locked in a cell!"

Kirkpatrick gasped, "Dick, have you gone mad? We need every friend at Washington we can get right now!"

"Mad?" Wentworth's voice rose. "Mad? No, I'm not mad! G-man Miller, so-called, is the Master! I'm going after him at once!"

Wentworth raced down the stairs and caught up Nita at the door of the city hall. He raced with her to a car and sent it hurtling northward through the city. Crowds still blocked their way, but as they sped farther north, the people thinned out and he could go faster. He saw Black Police cornered and captured by men in blue, and everywhere the faces of people were beginning to smile again. Oppression was lifting. And at the armory in the Bronx would come the ultimate victory....

"No, I can't be wrong," Wentworth was saying rapidly to Nita. "This supposed Miller tried to get you to tell the secrets of the camp while you were prisoners in Albany. His credentials seemed all right, but I'm willing to swear that, when we investigate, we'll find that a G-man named Miller was murdered and his papers taken."

He pointed out, "When he came blindfolded to our camp in the hills, he told us nothing that every official in the state didn't know by that time—that the President had ordered an election. He came to make sure that Whiting was saved, and that he didn't talk. Whiting must have known more than we thought or else have known things the importance of which he didn't recognize."

"But he testified for you at your trial," Nita urged. "He tried to make them let you go."

"But he failed," Wentworth said, "and because he had protested, you and the rest figured that Washington must know the full details and didn't make any effort to communicate with federal authorities. That was what he accomplished, besides diverting suspicion from himself."

He explained. "In the prison van, driving to the camp, Miller tapped out messages to me, apparently as a prisoner—trying to learn if I knew of any plans to liberate me. You notice that when we searched the camp for him, he was gone? That was because he was not really a prisoner. He didn't think there was any chance of my escape, so he had abandoned the role and left the camp. I realize that none of this evidence will stand in court, but it can be checked… as soon as we get the fingerprints of the real G-man from Washington."

HE BROKE off then as the armory came in sight over the crest of a hill. As he watched, men darted from the doorway and started off in all directions in cars and motorcycles. Nita's hand flew to Wentworth's arm, and he felt the elation suddenly go out of him. He did not need to ask the meaning of those suddenly dispersing men, but hoping against hope, he rushed into the building.

He found the cell where Miller had been prisoner. Lying in the corridor before it were the bodies of four men, terribly mangled by a bursting grenade. Two others had been shot… but the cell was empty. Miller was gone.

On the metal bench inside, Wentworth found a brief note addressed to him:

> Greetings to the Spider. Sorry I can't remain for more intimate converse with you, but I'm afraid this role has outlived its usefulness. Yours the victory today… Mine, tomorrow!
>
> THE MASTER.

On the bench lay the credentials of G-man Miller. That was all.

Sailor Joe came hurriedly into the cell. "I got orders from Captain Kirkpatrick, sir," he said, "and sent men to put the chains on Miller. Then I heard that explosion and, when I got here, Miller was gone! What the hell does it mean—begging your pardon, Miss, I'm sure."

Wentworth said heavily, "It means the Master has been too smart for us, once more, Joe. And while he's at large, we stand small chance of conquering the state and putting an end to the tyrannies of the Master and his men. We can look for trouble at once."

"But, Dick," Nita cried. "You've won a splendid victory. If you work fast, you can beat him out."

"We will work fast," Wentworth said grimly. "And perhaps we'll win. It won't be for lack of trying." He looked down again at the note left by the Master, and his lips moved....

"Yours the victory today. Mine, tomorrow!"

POPULAR HERO PULPS AVAILABLE NOW:

ACE G-MAN
- ❑ #1: The Suicide Squad Reports for Death $14.95
- ❑ #2: Coffins for the Suicide Squad $14.95

OPERATOR 5
- ❑ #1: The Masked Invasion $13.95
- ❑ #2: The Invisible Empire $13.95
- ❑ #3: The Yellow Scourge $13.95
- ❑ #4: The Melting Death $13.95
- ❑ #5: Cavern of the Damned $13.95
- ❑ #6: Master of Broken Men $13.95
- ❑ #7: Invasion of the Dark Legions $13.95
- ❑ #8: The Green Death Mists $13.95
- ❑ #9: Legions of Starvation $13.95
- ❑ #10: The Red Invader $13.95
- ❑ #11: The League of War-Monsters $13.95
- ❑ #12: The Army of the Dead $13.95
- ❑ #13: March of the Flame Marauders $13.95
- ❑ #14: Blood Reign of the Dictator $13.95
- ❑ #15: Invasion of the Yellow Warlords $13.95
- ❑ #16: Legions of the Death Master $13.95
- ❑ #17: Hosts of the Flaming Death $13.95
- ❑ #18: Invasion of the Crimson Death Cult $13.95
- ❑ #19: Attack of the Blizzard Men $13.95
- ❑ #20: Scourge of the Invisible Death $13.95
- ❑ #21: Raiders of the Red Death $13.95
- ❑ #22: War-Dogs of the Green Destroyer $13.95
- ❑ #23: Rockets From Hell $13.95
- ❑ #24: War-Masters from the Orient $13.95
- ❑ #25: Crime's Reign of Terror $13.95
- ❑ #26: Death's Ragged Army $13.95
- ❑ #27: Patriots' Death Battalion $13.95
- ❑ #28: The Bloody Forty-five Days $13.95
- ❑ #29: America's Plague Battalions $13.95
- ❑ #30: Liberty's Suicide Legions $13.95
- ❑ #31: Siege of the Thousand Patriots $13.95
- ❑ #32: Patriots' Death March $14.95
- ❑ #33: Revolt of the Lost Legions $14.95
- ❑ **NEW:** #34: Drums of Destruction $14.95

CAPTAIN COMBAT
- ❑ #1: The Sky Beast of Berlin $13.95
- ❑ #2: Red Wings For the Blood Battalion $13.95
- ❑ #3: Low Ceiling For Nazi Hell Hawks $13.95

DUSTY AYRES AND HIS BATTLE BIRDS
- ❑ #1: Black Lightning! $13.95
- ❑ #2: Crimson Doom $13.95
- ❑ #3: The Purple Tornado $13.95
- ❑ #4: The Screaming Eye $13.95
- ❑ #5: The Green Thunderbolt $13.95
- ❑ #6: The Red Destroyer $13.95
- ❑ #7: The White Death $13.95
- ❑ #8: The Black Avenger $13.95
- ❑ #9: The Silver Typhoon $13.95
- ❑ #10: The Troposphere F-S $13.95
- ❑ #11: The Blue Cyclone $13.95
- ❑ #12: The Tesla Raiders $13.95

MAVERICKS
- ❑ #1: Five Against the Law $12.95
- ❑ #2: Mesquite Manhunters $12.95
- ❑ #3: Bait for the Lobo Pack $12.95
- ❑ #4: Doc Grimson's Outlaw Posse $12.95
- ❑ #5: Charlie Parr's Gunsmoke Cure $12.95

THE MYSTERIOUS WU FANG
- ❑ #1: The Case of the Six Coffins $12.95
- ❑ #2: The Case of the Scarlet Feather $12.95
- ❑ #3: The Case of the Yellow Mask $12.95
- ❑ #4: The Case of the Suicide Tomb $12.95
- ❑ #5: The Case of the Green Death $12.95
- ❑ #6: The Case of the Black Lotus $12.95
- ❑ #7: The Case of the Hidden Scourge $12.95

THE SECRET 6
- ❑ #1: The Red Shadow $13.95
- ❑ #2: House of Walking Corpses $13.95
- ❑ #3: The Monster Murders $13.95
- ❑ #4: The Golden Alligator $13.95

CAPTAIN ZERO
- ❑ #1: City of Deadly Sleep $13.95
- ❑ #2: The Mark of Zero! $13.95
- ❑ #3: The Golden Murder Syndicate $13.95